THE FINAL INSTALMENT

Oswald Trent is an actor who has never quite made the grade. While on tour in Canada he is taken up by Joey Rossi, who takes him on gambling junkets where Oswald learns how to collect money illicitly. When a mob war breaks out, Oswald flees to London where he sets up in partnership with experienced fence Rufus Whittaker. Meanwhile, Sam Harris and old flame Carrie Newland are looking for Oswald in connection with a jewel robbery, and a hatchet-man from the States is after him. Oswald goes into hiding – but when Sam and Carrie get to him it is too late...

THE FINAL INSTALMENT

THE FINAL INSTALMENT

by

Michael Cronin

Dales Large Print Books
Long Preston, North Yorkshire,
BD23 4ND, England.

British Library Cataloguing in Publication Data.

Cronin, Michael
        The final instalment.

        A catalogue record of this book is
        available from the British Library

        ISBN   978-1-84262-601-6 pbk

First published in Great Britain 1976 by Robert Hale & Co.

Copyright © Michael Cronin 1976

The moral right of the author has been asserted

Published in Large Print 2008 by arrangement with
MIchael Cronin, care of Watson, Little Ltd.

Dales Large Print is an imprint of Library Magna Books Ltd.

Printed and bound in Great Britain by
T.J. (International) Ltd., Cornwall, PL28 8RW

PART ONE

1

Oswald Trent was the son of a parson in a Surrey village, and after attending a nearby public school at greatly reduced fees, he set out to make his way in the theatre.

He had a long sensitive face, a high forehead with soft wavy brown hair, an athletic figure, a good voice, and enough intelligence to take direction provided not too much subtlety was expected of him, since his range was limited. He was very English and correct, and obviously a gentleman. He always thought of himself as the Leslie Howard type.

If he had been old enough to have appeared in the Thirties he might have fashioned himself a reasonable stage career in drawing-room dramas and romantic comedies, getting by on his looks and style, and the appeal of that cultured voice. But in the theatre of the Fifties and the Sixties the kind of parts he might have coped with adequately were just not coming along any more, and he didn't have a big enough name for producers to take much of a chance on him in other roles.

He had a few walk-on parts in some short-lived West End productions, and some seasons in repertory companies in remote areas where he made little significant impact – just another name in small print on the bills.

He tried films without ever landing a featured role. He didn't photograph well and he couldn't forget that he had been on in the West End, which made him superior to the riff-raff he had to associate with in the studio. Nobody was terribly impressed by that lovely voice of his, except as a comic relief and an invitation to parody.

His private life had been no more successful either. After the normal succession of short-lived entanglements incidental to his way of life, he had married a statuesque blonde with family connections rather above his level – gentlemen farmers, stockbrokers, company directors. Doris was also some four years older than Oswald, and considerably sharper when it came down to hard facts. She had a good Cambridge degree, and a very promising perch in one of the better advertising agencies.

She was no raving beauty, just a healthy uncomplicated young woman, with a clear idea of what she thought she wanted out of life. And very soon after she had married Oswald she decided that he had been a bad bargain. They had little to say to each other, and within a year she was paying most of the bills since she was earning three times as much as he did.

If they had been really in love it wouldn't have mattered all that much, but their sex life had become perfunctory, and Doris was quite content when he was away from home on one of his infrequent tours. They bickered in bed and out of it, and their reconciliations became more and more temporary and artificial.

The final split came when she discovered that he had been using her money to pay his debts to the bookies. He had always been a gambler, and in a desperate attempt to show her that he could make money as well he had been plunging heavily. Nothing had come up and he was in a mess.

The flat was in her name, and she had bought most of the furniture. With unlady-like vehemence she told him he could pack his bags and get out; she wanted no more of him; he was shiftless and a cheat, a complete cad when it came down to it – just as her family had warned her; absolutely untrust-worthy when it came to money, her money.

A gentleman to the bitter end, Oswald told her what a crashing bore she had become, and another marriage had gone *phut* for good.

He spent some futile weeks attending auditions, offering himself for parts he knew he hadn't a hope in hell of getting just so as to keep in touch with what was going on in the business, listening in to the gossip of who was rumoured to be casting and for what, doing the rounds indefatigably – 'don't call us, we'll call you'…

He still had the remains of a good wardrobe, and the style had not yet deserted him; he had never lacked assurance, and now he was ready to try almost anything with a pay packet.

Eventually he talked his way into a company that was being collected for an extended tour in Canada. It was something of a come-down, he was to start as assistant stage manager with the promise of some parts later on – it was the kind of deal normally offered to a student fresh out of drama school, a starry-eyed stage-struck novice. If times had been better Oswald would have been insulted at the derisory proposition.

But he was sure that his day had to come;

there would be the lucky break and he would show these youngsters how Coward and Rattigan and Pinter and so forth should be played. It had to happen.

It didn't. None of the company dropped out even for a couple of performances; they remained disgustingly fit and healthy; the stage manager used him as little more than an office boy, and consistently ignored any brilliant suggestion he cared to make to improve the company's impact. Oswald found him a stroppy young man with no manners and no real feel for the theatre. Whenever he took his complaints to the producer, which he did fairly frequently, he got little joy: the company was doing very good business and was receiving excellent notices wherever it played, so if Oswald Trent was not happy in his work the remedy was in his own hands.

Furthermore, the producer also warned him not to mess about with the younger actresses, since they did not welcome his attentions; it was bad for morale and he ought to know better at his age. So for Oswald the whole thing was going very sour.

It was bad enough to be so ignored professionally when he knew he could do a better job than any of the so-called leads, it was an additional hurt to be told that the girls thought of him as a dirty old man – he had only slept with one of them, Carol Hugesson, and it had been at her open invitation; she was twenty one and certainly no shy virgin. In fact, she had told him he had given her a lovely time, and he had been waiting to repeat the treatment.

It was a conspiracy, that was what it was. He really didn't have a friend in the whole company. He was never going to be allowed a chance to show what a talent he had, and it was galling to be treated as a pompous has-been, a middle-aged errand boy.

A chance acquaintance in a hotel bar in Hamilton, Ontario, persuaded him that he would do better in the States, Boston, for instance, where the genuine English style still counted.

The friendly character in question was a Johnny Scimona, about Oswald's age but with nothing of his looks; he was fat and swarthy and coarse; a second-generation Italian-American who had evidently made good. A lavish spender, he was, he said, sort of in show business himself. He had an interest in some clubs where they put on floor shows, around Boston and Rhode Island.

'I'm always on the look out for the right

kind of guy to fill in as MC, somebody with a bit of class who can deliver a line and put the folks in a good mood, know what I mean?' Johnny Scimona waved a pudgy hand. 'If you can think fast on your feet, crack a few gags – nothing too blue, mind you, I don't go for that, just sophisticated family entertainment, if you follow me. It ain't Shakespeare, that's for sure, but it pays. Would you be interested, mister, if I had an opening?'

Oswald said he was more than interested. The company was happy to release him from his contract, since it saved the producer from the unpleasant duty of giving him the bullet. And two days later Johnny Scimona was driving him over the border in a large white Cadillac. Oswald Trent's luck had turned. He saw a glittering future opening up; it could lead him anywhere, right to the top.

When they got to Boston, Johnny Scimona summoned Bennie Munck who looked after the entertainment end of the Scimona enterprises, and Bennie was less than enthusiastic at the prospect of finding something suitable for this new character the boss had picked up.

'You got any track record as emm-cee any

place?' Bennie demanded.

'Not exactly,' said Oswald Trent. 'But I am an actor with a fairly wide experience, my dear chap. West End productions in London, quite a few films–'

–'Forget it,' said Bennie. 'I'm talking about show-biz, our kind of show-biz–'

'Fit him in, Bennie,' said Johnny Scimona and it was the boss speaking.

'Okay,' said Bennie gloomily. 'There's a slot at the motel for a compere. They'll murder him for sure.'

Thus, with the minimum of rehearsal time, Oswald was stuck out there with a mike, allegedly to introduce the cabaret turns at a motel complex outside Worcester, Massachusetts, where he died the death twice nightly.

There was no actual script to guide him, just a gag book with material of graded shades of blue, and some marginal notes of blush-making effectiveness from previous performers. Oswald studied it all. He had to in order to survive, and Johnny Scimona was paying him three hundred and fifty dollars a week plus free accommodation at the motel.

With an ease that surprised even himself, he began to pick up the speed of the so-called show. He was imitative and adaptable, and he was learning to trade insult for insult with his fellow-performers on stage, and with the noisy audience when necessary.

He was picking up the trick of thinking fast on his feet, as Johnny Scimona had put it, and his extensive vocabulary came in very useful – he had more words at his command, polysyllabic words, and no matter how raucous the interruption he was learning to keep his cool.

Johnny Scimona's warning about being careful over the dirty stuff apparently didn't mean a thing, unless the management gave the tip that the law was out front and then they cleaned the patter up, but not too much. There was excellent liaison, because the manager knew when the police could be expected long before they showed, and everybody was happy.

Johnny Scimona had pull.

After some weeks at the motel, Oswald realised that he had created something of a character for himself. He was the cultured English-type gentleman who could put over a blue gag as though it had popped out accidentally, and the bogus innocent 'business' he got through with the strip-teasing dancers on a stacked Saturday night had the cash customers falling around. His timing was superb. And quite naughty.

The guy was turning out to be a real riot in that snappy custom-built suit with the white tie and tails and the black cane with a silver knob, and that cane came in pretty handy with the strippers when the invitation was to 'get 'em off' – Oswald Trent couldn't sing or dance worth a damn, but he was sharp and quick, and they never caught him off balance.

There was no dignity about what he was doing, and it had nothing to do with the theatre, but he was enjoying the fringe benefits; the free accommodation left him with some spending money in his pocket, and since the word had got around that he had a connection with Johnny Scimona he found that his credit was unexpectedly good. The motel never presented any bill for his drinks, and there was never any bother about getting the loan of a staff car. So life could have been far more rugged.

He was featured on the billing now: *Oswald Trent. Esquire. The Genuine Gentleman. From London. England.*

It was shameful and so vulgar, really. But Johnny Scimona had raised his pay by a hundred dollars, and there was the promise of a television spot one day soon.

Johnny dropped in now and then to catch the show. He was always given VIP treatment, with his own table and express service. With him there would be a young man in a dark suit who sat a little apart and drank fruit juice and watched the audience, not the show.

Johnny never introduced him, and the people who came to join Johnny at his table never made any attempt to draw the young man into the conversation. They all seemed to be heavy spenders, most of them with Italian names, and the women with them were often young and quite gorgeous. Party girls.

Ossie had guessed as much even before the motel manager warned him to keep away. By now Ossie had in fact guessed a lot, about Johnny Scimona and his associates. They all had money to throw around and no recognisable occupations. They had power, and their own hierarchy, and it was clear that Johnny Scimona had plenty of rank because nobody seemed ready to question his opinions.

When Ossie put it to the motel manager he got a very quick reaction:

'Mafia? Boy, that's a word we don't use around here. If you want to stay healthy you better forget that kind of talk, people don't like it.'

It was in the middle of the morning in the manager's office behind the main restaurant; there was nobody else about, but all the same, Charlie Stryker, the manager, was nervous. They had become pretty good friends.

'Don't tell me any secrets,' said Ossie with a grin. 'I can guess. So Johnny Scimona is one of those gang bosses and that silent young man who comes with him is his bodyguard. How quaint. Just like in the pictures.'

'You better keep your funny cracks for the stage,' said Charlie Stryker. 'You never heard a word from me.'

'The Cosa Nostra, well well,' said Ossie. 'I never expected to find myself working for that lot. I must give it my closer attention.'

'You do that you'll end up very dead,' said Charlie.

'The mystique of violence,' said Ossie, 'A fascinating study – I've never really known a professional gangster, are they as sub-human as report has it?'

'Listen to me,' said Charlie, 'if Johnny Scimona gives him the nod that young feller in the dark suit will crease you for good, and he'll never ask Johnny why. No fuss, you just won't be around any more.'

'A delightful prospect,' said Ossie. 'If you are trying to scare me, Charlie, you are doing very well.'

'Just watch yourself,' said Charlie.

'Does this unfriendly character have a name?' said Ossie.

'Vince Flemmi. He had an older brother, Steve. Used to be the top hit-man for Vincent Charlie Teresa. You must have heard of Fat Man Teresa. He was the Number Two to Raymond Patriarca, there was a book about him.'

'I missed it,' said Ossie.

'Vince Flemmi is bad news,' said Charlie.

'I must remember to have nothing to do with him,' said Ossie. 'I don't like his pedigree. I take it that a hit-man is a professional killer?' F/0233110

'What else?' said Charlie.

'What about the police?' said Ossie.

Charlie just smiled. And rubbed finger and thumb together.

'It's organised,' he said. 'If a guy like Vince Flemmi gets pulled in it'll have to be on suspicion – there won't be any evidence and there sure as hell won't be any witnesses, so he gets sprung. It happens all the time. Listen, don't you know anything?'

'I'm learning fast,' said Ossie.

'If Johnny Scimona ever heard you were asking about him and his business, he would not like it at all.'

'Are you going to tell him?' said Ossie, and it was not a flippant question.

Charlie Stryker spread his hands. 'I got a good living here. The way I see it, buddie, you're just passing through.'

'Precisely,' said Ossie. 'A strolling player.'

'So keep strolling, that's my advice to you,' said Charlie.

'In due course,' said Ossie. 'There seems to be a lot of easy money floating around here, and that interests me. You know, I always thought the Mafia days were over and done with.'

'If you believe that,' said Charlie, 'you ought to see a head shrinker. Nobody on the inside used that Mafia name, they never really did – it got all that bad publicity. The same with Cosa Nostra. In this territory it's the New England Office, and you won't hear anybody shouting that aloud either, not if they know what's good for them. The one thing they can do without is publicity. All the Murder Incorporated crap, that was bad for business. It blows up every now and then, of course, and the cops have to go through the motions and pull in a few little guys who don't matter.'

'The situation is familiar,' said Ossie.

'The money that comes in from the rackets is laundered,' said Charlie. 'They can afford to buy expert brains to invest the cash in legitimate enterprises so that the revenue guys can't trace it back. Real estate all over the country, hotels and apartment blocks, respectable business corporations – even a little joint like this, I show a nice profit and I keep proper accounts, Johnny Scimona would have my hide if I didn't.'

'Is he all that big in the organisation?' said Ossie. 'I guessed he was some kind of gangster some time ago, but to be honest I rather like him, he's treated me very well.'

'He has respect, as they put it,' said Charlie. 'He has a good place in the family. He's my boss and I don't have any complaints, and in case you're thinking it – I'm not in the mob and you can believe it or not.'

'If you were you wouldn't be telling me this,' said Ossie.

'Lots of guys like me,' said Charlie. 'I don't see what I don't have to see, and I don't hear what is none of my business. You got it?'

'Very discreet,' said Ossie.

'When Johnny Scimona comes in here and hands me a cash bonus I take it,' said Charlie. 'So maybe they say it's dirty money, I wouldn't know. I keep my nose clean and I can't afford to be fussy.'

'A sensible attitude,' said Ossie.

'You have to take things as they are,' said Charlie. 'Wherever there's money to be picked up you'll find the mob guys are around. Gambling, hijacking, cheque frauds, robbery, prostitution, all the angles in the protection racket, loansharking – the lot, if it pays off high they run it. A couple of years ago a government investigator reckoned the New England take was grossing over seven hundred million. Maybe it's not that heavy now, that was when Patriarca and old Enrico Tameleo were the bosses, they're not around any more, but the business hasn't closed up. There's plenty of suckers and plenty of money about. The organisation works, and don't let anybody tell you different. Now will you get the hell away from me before we both get ourselves into bad trouble.'

'No trouble from me,' said Ossie. 'I have a powerful instinct for self-preservation. Like you, I intend to live until I'm a very old man, and in reasonable comfort.'

'So watch yourself,' said Charlie. 'You don't have anything like this in your little country. It's organised all the way, buddie, and don't you ever forget it.'

'A most entertaining talk,' said Ossie. 'I appreciate it, Charlie.'

'I never said a word, now beat it,' said Charlie.

2

For some months Oswald Trent continued to do his stuff at the motel with reasonable success. He was being very careful not to give Johnny Scimona any cause to put him under examination for any reason whatsoever. Nobody was to have a second thought about Ossie: he put his act over and he got the right laughs, and then he was ready to fade into the background, unless Johnny required his presence at the VIP table, where he would be discretion itself.

Johnny thought he was okay and said so frequently. With no inclination for the celibate life, Ossie had made a friendly arrangement with Olivia Haldstedt who ran the catering at the motel; she was a divorcée of mature years, a genuine ash blonde who had looked after herself; she had very good legs and neat hips, and a refreshing appetite for bed-time activities.

Ossie found her eminently satisfactory; she made him feel ten years younger, and her cabin at the motel was convenient to his, so there was no need to make their association too open. Olivia had ideas about not being taken for another broad; she had her reputation to think of, and Ossie was supposed to be a gentleman.

Charlie knew all about it, but it didn't hurt business, so it was okay.

It should have been an ideal set-up, but Ossie had money in his pocket, and he was moving in an atmosphere where gambling was the norm and not the exception. There was no regular action going on at the motel, but there were plenty of games to be found elsewhere, and New England is not short of race tracks. Also Olivia liked a day at the races, and like a proper little lady she was happy to gamble with Ossie's money. If she came up it was hers, naturally. Fun money.

The result was inevitable. Ossie found

himself in the red, and he owed money to guys who were not of Johnny Scimona's family and who were thus not inclined to give him any favours, like time to pay and so forth.

It became really serious when a pair of hard guys in a truck ran Ossie and Olivia off the highway in broad daylight and advised Ossie that he had twenty four hours to come up with the full payment or he would get both legs broken and the broad would maybe have her pretties carved and how did they like that.

Charlie Stryker came to the rescue. He advanced Ossie enough to get himself in the clear; he would take it out of Ossie's pay and it would keep Ossie short for quite some time.

'Johnny Scimona will know about it,' said Charlie. 'He won't like it, usually he reckons to look after his own people, but you broke a serious rule – when you lose you pay, and you don't squeal. If you can't pay you don't play. Now you've embarrassed Johnny Scimona.'

'It won't happen again,' said Ossie.

'Like hell it won't,' said Charlie. 'If you got to toss your money away make sure it's in the right company next time, come and ask me and I'll put you wise.'

'So the games were rigged,' said Ossie. 'I suspected as much, but they were pretty slick about it, I couldn't spot anything.'

'Don't be stupid all your life,' said Charlie. 'You don't expect to sit in on a card game with guys you don't know and get a fair shake. I once saw Yonkers Joe Silistrino operate in a casino in Miami. He was the top mechanic of them all – he could switch in a stacked deck right there in front of the suckers and they'd never see a thing. He had a real talent for manipulating a deck of cards.'

'I'm glad I never met him across a table,' said Ossie.

'You play for peanuts, buddie,' said Charlie. 'You'll never be in the Silistrino league. Get wise to yourself – you got plenty going for you here, so don't foul it up.'

Several days later Vince Flemmi arrived at the motel in the middle of the morning. He was alone and he was driving the air-conditioned Cadillac. He found Charlie and Ossie taking their morning coffee in Charlie's office, and he entered without bothering to knock.

'Boss wants you,' he said to Ossie. 'C'mon.'

And he walked out and back to the car.

'Here's where I get my wrist slapped,' said Ossie.

'My best wishes,' said Charlie. 'When he sends for you it is not good, my friend.'

'I'll grovel,' said Ossie, feeing anything but light of heart.

There was an uneasy ride into Boston, with Vince Flemmi saying never a word, while Ossie reflected on the awkwardness that might lie ahead, and trusted to his natural glibness to get him back into a good repute with Johnny Scimona.

They stopped at a large warehouse building where evidently some legitimate business was being carried on, with trucks loading and unloading goods in cartons. It was all being done quite openly.

They went round to a side door and up a short flight of stairs and along a corridor where they could hear the clacking of typewriters and the allied noises of business being transacted. This time Vince Flemmi knocked at the door and nodded to Ossie to go in.

Johnny Scimona sat at a desk with some papers, talking briskly into a phone tucked into his shoulder to leave his hands free. He smiled at Ossie and indicated a chair.

Ossie sat and tried not to appear to be listening. It was mostly numbers and figures and some kind of business shorthand that meant nothing to him – consignments and deliveries and so forth.

When Johnny Scimona had finished he said, 'that clears me for the day, how about you and me going to the races at Suffolk Downs? You never been there yet with me.'

'I'd like nothing better,' said Ossie, relieved at the friendly atmosphere.

'Let's go,' said Johnny, getting up.

'There's a slight difficulty,' said Ossie. 'I wasn't expecting this, as a matter of fact I haven't much cash with me–'

Johnny Scimona unlocked a drawer and took out a cash box which he unlocked and pushed across the desk. 'Be my guest.'

'That's very generous of you,' said Ossie.

'It's only money.' A surprising comment from Johnny Scimona.

Ossie took five hundred. The box held nothing but one-hundred-dollar bills, all crisp and new.

'I thought you were a betting man,' said Johnny Scimona. 'You won't get far with chicken feed like that.'

Ossie smiled nervously. 'My ambitions are modest. I don't want to get in too deep.'

'Chicken feed,' said Johnny. He picked up five more bills and passed them over. 'That makes it an even grand. You can't open with less than that, not when you come racing with me.'

'My luck hasn't been too good lately,' said Ossie, tucking the money into his wallet. 'It may be just chicken feed to you, but it's real money to me – I hope I can repay this loan before the day is over.'

Johnny Scimona gave him a blank look. 'I'll collect,' he announced.

Vince Flemmi drove them, with Johnny Scimona and Ossie in the back. After some desultory conversation, largely about the iniquitous state of American politics, of which Ossie knew very little, Johnny Scimona fell asleep, as quickly and as tidily as a cat napping on the rug in front of a fire, leaving his guest to watch the scenery sliding past, and Ossie couldn't forget the way he had said, 'I'll collect' – and that bundle of notes in his wallet became very important. It was easy to believe that nobody was permitted to owe money to Johnny Scimona for very long.

At the race track Johnny was wide awake, and on the way up to their places in the stand he was greeting a number of characters who appeared equally happy to see him – a wave of the hand, a nod and a quick word and maybe a laugh and a slap on a shoulder. And all the while Vince Flemmi was at his elbow.

Charlie Stryker had said Johnny had 'respect', and Ossie was seeing it work. Nobody jostled them, and their places in the stand were good ones.

They had a salad lunch in the restaurant supposedly reserved for owners and officials, and here Ossie noticed that Johnny Scimona didn't mingle quite so freely, and nobody came over to be introduced to his guest. This was one occasion when Vince Flemmi was not around, but he joined them as soon as they came out.

'A bit frigid in there I thought,' said Ossie.

'The bastards would like to bar me,' said Johnny Scimona, 'but they can never make anything stick. The hell with them, let's go racing.'

Ossie was expecting some inside information, but he was left to his own devices, and accordingly lost a hundred dollars on each of the first two races on the card, which slowed him up a little. Johnny Scimona didn't place a bet.

Ossie went down on the third race, fifty dollars this time, which meant a quarter of his stake money had gone. And still Johnny didn't visit the windows.

'All right,' said Ossie. 'What's happening?'

'Now listen good,' said Johnny Scimona softly. 'In the sixth, Gay Buccaneer – get your bundle on before the price shortens.'

Gay Buccaneer was listed at 20-1. With no form at all. Ossie hesitated.

'You fool around and you'll miss it,' said Johnny.

Ossie put five hundred on it. And wondered if he was cutting his own throat. He couldn't bear to watch the fifth race. He was watching the tote board instead, and a minute before the sixth race got under way Gay Buccaneer was down to 4-1.

'No sweat,' said Johnny Scimona.

Gay Buccaneer romped it by a clear six lengths pulling up. And Ossie collected over four thousand dollars.

'That's it,' said Johnny. 'Now we go home.'

In the car Ossie settled his debt. 'I ought to charge you for the inside information,' said Johnny.

'A fix I suppose?' said Ossie. 'That's the first time I've been in on one of those.'

'Just another banana race,' said Johnny. 'That's what we call them. Don't you have them in England?'

'Very rarely,' said Ossie. 'I didn't notice you doing any betting.'

'I use out of town bookmakers, the guys who don't know the fix is in. It wouldn't be smart to hit the home town boys. I did all right.'

'I'm sure you did,' said Ossie.

'Like printing your own money,' said Johnny.

'I begin to see why we weren't too popular back there in the restaurant,' said Ossie. 'You must be a marked man.'

'Doesn't worry me none,' said Johnny. 'They can suspect all they like when a long shot comes home like that, but they'll never be able to prove that Gay Buccaneer was juiced this afternoon. Right now they'll be checking the urine sample, but the one they got won't be the one they want – we call it switching the spit-box. It comes expensive and it takes a good organisation. You have to make sure you sweeten the right guy in the stables, and take care of the jockey, and you can't operate too often on the same track or the word gets around and there's too much heavy money on an outsider, so you don't get a price. Stands to reason, don't it?'

'Indeed it does,' said Ossie.

'It's a piece of business,' said Johnny, 'and it pays off big if you handle it right, you can never stop the suckers from gambling.'

'That's me,' said Ossie. 'I've never had the benefit of inside information before.'

'You getting the message?' said Johnny.

'A salutary lesson,' said Ossie. 'You can't win unless you happen to be on the inside. How does the owner come out of all this?'

Johnny Scimona nearly smiled. 'Maybe he's a dummy, he gets his cut, same as the physicians who pick up a nice piece of cash from supplying the stuff, stimulants or depressives ... old Doc Reilly from Charlestown, he could supply anything you wanted, for horses or dogs, made no difference, Charlie Reilly had it – at a price. Now button it up while I catch up on my sleep.'

'The next time I go racing,' said Ossie, 'I'll bear all this in mind.'

'The next time you aim to go racing,' said Johnny Scimona, 'do yourself a favour and stay home – you'll save money that way.' A few minutes later he was once more fast asleep, and he slept all the way back into Boston, a compact and tough little figure of a man who didn't look at all dangerous, when he was asleep. And he had the useful habit of being able to fall asleep at the drop of a hat. He was also reputed to be able to stay awake for days on end and on the ball all the time when a deal was going tricky or when some opposition had turned up unexpectedly. A hard man with a strong organisation behind him, and no shortage of money.

Oswald Trent had never been even remotely associated with an operator like Johnny Scimona before, and he already knew that he would have to be very very careful. He also knew there could be one hell of a lot of money coming his way if he made the right moves at the right time.

They didn't repeat their visit to the races. It had served its purpose, and Ossie was making an attempt to live almost within his means, which was something he hadn't tried for a number of years.

Sunday was his one free day and he normally expected to spend it with Olivia Haldstedt. They would get up late, and they might take her car for a drive out somewhere for a meal where they imagined they weren't known. Olivia knew the best places and she had a healthy appetite for food as well as sex. In his time Ossie had known plenty of women who were far less fun than Olivia.

She didn't pry into his past, and he didn't find it necessary to pretend to her that he had once been a big performer in London. She knew about Doris, of course, but naturally didn't spend any time thinking about her.

The way Olivia figured it, they had a dud marriage each behind them, and nobody was expected to go on paying for a mistake all their lives; everybody was entitled to a second chance.

She made Ossie happy, and he gave her plenty of loving as well. So they settled for that. It was a mutual thing, and nobody was going to get hurt because they both had too much sense.

About the matter of working for the mob, Olivia had the same view as Charlie Stryker – realistic neutrality. They were paying her well over the going rate for what she was expected to do, and she never had to do anything she didn't care about. It was strictly business and on the level as far as she was concerned.

And nobody who used the motel ever tried anything crude with her. There had been a guy once who tried some strong-arm stuff on her one night in her cabin, and when she wouldn't come across he got rough because he was a regular client and reckoned he had privileges with the hired help.

When Olivia complained it got the guy a load of grief on Johnny Scimona's personal orders – they chopped him where it hurt most so he wouldn't be getting fresh with any females any more.

There were plenty of worse places to work than Johnny Scimona's motel. You got a square deal as long as you didn't stick your nose in where it wasn't wanted.

One evening Charlie Stryker had a phone call and sent for Ossie.

'The man wants you tonight, Ossie,' he said. 'You have to report at the Carlton Country Club at ten. I just now had the word from Bennie Munck and if he knew what it was all about he wasn't telling me so don't ask.'

'What about my show here?' said Ossie.

'Buddie boy,' said Charlie, 'when Johnny Scimona sends for a guy that guy asks no stupid questions – he presents himself nice and respectable and waits for orders. Have you been getting yourself into hock with the bookies again? I thought we straightened that out.'

'My conscience is clear, almost,' said Ossie. 'I haven't placed a bet or touched a deck of cards in a month or so.'

'Maybe Johnny's going to give you a medal,' said Charlie. 'We'll do our best to manage without you tonight. You've never been to the Carlton before, have you?'

'On my kind of money?' said Ossie. 'I'm not that ambitious.'

'Johnny Scimona has a big slice of it,' said Charlie. 'A lot of money circulates around that place.'

'I'll have both hands out,' said Ossie.

'Keep yourself tidy,' said Charlie. 'Don't get too smart with the man.'

'I'll be on my knees,' said Ossie. 'No flowers by request.'

'Ten on the dot,' said Charlie.

3

The Carlton Country Club was a comparatively recent venture, located in the wooded countryside some miles outside the Boston city limits. A heap of money had been poured into it in an attempt to rival the other establishments in the same line of business, the ones that prided themselves on being exclusive and high-class, where one could be sure to meet only solid citizens of the utmost probity and financial standing – one's own kind of people, in fact.

Although it had much to offer, the Carlton had still to make the grade with the really reputable old-moneyed families. They professed to find it vulgar, and suspected, with good reason, that much of the money in evidence there had a bad history. One heard unpleasant stories, and the people one might meet there were not quite the right kind – they had too much money to throw around, and they did it without taste. Wild parties and gambling for high stakes – not a good atmosphere.

However, the Carlton was flourishing in its own fashion, and the original investors were getting a very handsome return on their money.

The amenities were extensive and well presented, and a patron would need to be very stuffy indeed or half-dead not to find something there to engage his attention.

You could play golf or tennis or squash, with professional coaches to put you right;

you could ride or swim – two pools, one inside and one outdoor and both heated. For the less energetic there was a restaurant with an ambitious menu that was seldom called upon to justify itself because most of the customers didn't bother with it. There were bars and lounges and a dance floor with some pretty wild music by a resident group.

In an annexe there was the casino where the heavy action took place and the real profits were made; entry to the top room was restricted to those whose credit rating was sound, and even when the game wasn't rigged the house reckoned to take seventeen per cent of the stakes, creamed off the top before anybody else got anything. The casino staff were aces at their work, and nobody ever tried twice to put anything over on them, and nobody squawked – not more than once.

This was the big operation that made all the rest of it possible.

Over the casino were the private suites. If your contacts were okay and you felt like it, there were some sophisticated ladies who looked nothing like the hookers they were and who would accommodate you discreetly and expensively.

41

There were occasional stag-nights when reinforcements would have to be brought in, but they were exceptions, and the Carlton Country Club was not anxious to be known far and wide as just another sporting-house.

All you needed was money.

There were acres of landscaped grounds, and a high wall to keep out the trash who didn't have the dollars to join.

A few minutes before the appointed time Oswald Trent pulled up at the ornate flood-lit gates; they were closed, and a uniformed security guard stood on the inside and watched him stop; the guard wore a khaki battle-dress, with a peaked cap and a shiny black belt and a holster. He looked young and tough.

He came out through the side gate. 'You a member?' he said.

'No,' said Ossie. 'I'm here to see Mr Johnny Scimona. I am Oswald Trent.'

The guard checked a list he pulled out of his pocket. '

'Okay,' he said, 'just keep to the drive, mister.'

The gates were opened and Ossie drove in. The whole place was lit up like a city street. There were flood-lit hard tennis courts where a couple of games were still in progress.

He was looking for a place to park when a car-hop arrived and took over. The guard must have phoned from the gate, because a young man in a cream dinner jacket appeared on the scene and held out his hand and said, 'Evening, Mr Trent, nice to have you with us. I'm Pete Fallon, Johnny says to make yourself at home, he hopes to be with you right away.'

They went up into the main hall; it was all very lush, like a Hollywood set from the extravagant days. Fred Astaire and the nimble Ginger could have done their routines up and down those wide stairs.

'Quite a place,' said Ossie.

'Glad you like it,' said Pete Fallon. 'We aim to please. I kind of keep an eye on things.'

'It does you credit,' said Ossie.

'Nice feller,' said Fallon, touching Ossie's arm. 'You fancy a drink while we wait?'

'A friendly suggestion,' said Ossie.

They took a table near a long bar, where they had a view of the comings and goings. Ossie had Scotch, it was tolerable, just. Pete Fallon had coke. Ossie thought he spotted one or two men he recognised – people who had been at the motel with Johnny Scimona, or at the race track at Suffolk Downs. There were some attractive women around – Johnny Scimona's associates always had attractive women in their company, prestige symbols.

When Fallon heard that Ossie came from London, England, he wanted to talk about the old Colony Club there.

'I hear that was just about the top,' he said. 'Real class.'

'A bit too rich for my blood,' said Ossie. 'I wasn't ever a member, but I've been there once or twice.'

'Meyer Lansky and Dino Cellini,' said Pete Fallon reverently, 'they had it all going for them – imagine having a guy like George Raft as your front-man.'

'They deported him,' said Ossie.

'Too bad,' said Fallon. 'He had style, you can't put a cash price on genuine style … we could do with some of that around here – and you shouldn't quote me on that.'

'I wouldn't think of it,' said Ossie. He refused another drink. He had been summoned for an interview with Johnny Scimona for purposes as yet unknown, and he was thinking he would need to be sober and in his right mind.

After a while Pete Fallon excused himself because he had things to do. In the meanwhile Oswald Trent was the guest of the management.

So Ossie did some wandering around. In the indoor swimming pool a couple of youngsters were still exercising, up and down the length of the pool, very dedicated and serious; a boy and a girl, teenagers, probably brother and sister; the girl was easily the better of the two.

Along the end of the patio he ventured a glance into the casino annexe, and his arrival aroused the interest of a large young man in a dinner jacket who just happened to be lounging there by the door. He gave Ossie a half-smile.

'Just looking,' said Ossie.

The room was crowded, as many women as men; blue cigar smoke curled over the lights; the hushed concentration of the gamblers at their tables, like a congregation in church, absorbed in the action; the agile silent waiters ferrying the drinks about to encourage the losers to endure their losses.

The young man in the dinner jacket had moved up alongside Ossie. 'Small stakes in here,' he said softly. 'Nothing too serious, just a little fun, y'know – nobody has to get in too deep, but if you're looking for some real action–'

45

'Not me,' said Ossie. 'I'm not even a member.'

The young man's smile became fixed. 'That so? Just looking, you said? Then you'd better go look someplace else.'

Ossie nodded and withdrew, and the young man came to the door and watched him depart. The Carlton would no doubt have a number of careful young men like that one on its payroll; he probably had a little gun snugly fitted under that dinner jacket. It was a sobering thought, and it reminded Ossie just where he was. Nobody at the motel ever had to carry a gun, except Charlie Stryker when he was handling the cash. It would be different here.

Pete Fallon caught up with him. 'Sorry to keep you hanging around. Johnny's free now.'

They went along a corridor behind the casino, and through a door with the uncompromising sign – *Keep Out. Staff Only.* And Fallon had to unlock it. They were entering the administration area. The corridor was brilliantly lit and thickly carpeted, and where it turned there was a guard like the one at the main gate, sitting with his chair tilted and a girlie magazine in his lap. He nodded at them and said nothing.

Nobody was going to be allowed to take any liberties at the Carlton Country Club.

At the end of the corridor they went into a room that served as a waiting-room for the principal office inside; there were filing cabinets, a covered typewriter, some padded chairs; the lights were on and the room was empty.

They went through into the main office. There was a glass-topped desk, a pair of deep lounging chairs, a bronze carpet wall-to-wall, a phone and an inter-com on the desk. There were no windows and there was nobody waiting for them there.

There were two doors in the wall behind the desk, one of them was partly open.

Pete Fallon said, 'He'll be with you right away, make yourself at home, see you around.' Then he went out.

It was now some fifty minutes past the time he had been summoned to meet Johnny Scimona. Ossie lit a cigarette. He felt de-flated, and just a little irritated. Through the open door he heard odd sounds, slapping sounds, and the occasional grunt.

Johnny Scimona having himself a slice of sex while he kept his visitor waiting? That would be a bit much even for a character like Johnny.

The slapping sounds continued provocatively. Ossie drifted across, after all, the door was ajar, so they couldn't accuse him of eaves-dropping. He would close the door noisily, which might remind Johnny Scimona and whoever he had in there with him that sex should be a private thing.

But he peeped inside first – who wouldn't? Johnny Scimona lay on his belly on a rubbing couch with his head pillowed on his folded arms, there was a towel draped across his buttocks. There were tufts of dark hair on his shoulders. The room smelt of rubbing oil and talc and male sweat.

A middle-aged woman in a short white wrap-over coat was working on Johnny's neck muscles with a vigorous rhythm like a drummer in a band. She was a handsome near-white woman, frowning and professional, and from her sturdy build she looked able to toss Johnny Scimona over her shoulder if he put a hand where it shouldn't be.

So much for the sex-orgy.

The masseuse looked up and saw Ossie. Without breaking her tempo she said, 'Be coupla minutes, mister. Almost through here.'

Johnny Scimona swivelled his head round,

saw Ossie, and said nothing. Ossie closed the door. He had smoked another cigarette before Johnny appeared.

He wore dark slacks and a white shirt with no tie. He sat behind the desk and rolled his shoulders like a boxer flexing his muscles. He offered no apology for the delay.

'You been round the place,' he said. 'You like it?'

'It looks very prosperous,' said Ossie.

'A money-spinner,' said Johnny. 'I brought you here to make you a little proposition. The club is doing okay money-wise, what we have to do now is give it that extra touch of class which we don't have. You follow me?'

'You don't mean you're going respectable?' said Ossie.

'I wouldn't take it that far,' said Johnny. 'I want a guy with a good personality, a guy who can handle the social stuff – make the suckers feel good, especially the women, know what I mean? Kind of raise the tone of the place, a guy with good manners who knows how to keep the public sweet without having to kick them in the teeth – we got plenty of muscle around here already.'

'So I noticed,' said Ossie. 'I thought Pete Fallon was your manager here.'

'He's smart with figures,' said Johnny. 'He's not so good with people, gets in too many fights with the help – no tact, is all. He'll handle the business end, I'm here every other night and he'll operate on my say-so. Pete won't give you no headache.'

Ossie smiled. 'You're being a bit quick. I don't know that I'm interested, and I quite like the job I've got.'

'We just sold the motel,' said Johnny. 'A syndicate of new guys from Long Island, they just bought it. They aim to tear most of it down and build a hyper-market. There'll be no job for you there.'

'I see,' said Ossie. 'I'll have to think it over.'

'Give you five minutes,' said Johnny Scimona. 'Social director at the Carlton pays a grand a week and your pick of the staff cottages. If it works out we might throw in a percentage of the take after six months.'

'I'm not altogether clear what I'll have to do,' said Ossie. 'I'm supposed to be an entertainer, an actor – this might be a little out of my line.'

'Plenty going for you,' said Johnny. 'You got the words and you look okay, and you got more brains than most of the show-biz folk I meet.'

'I'm glad to hear it,' said Ossie.

'And I'll be around to steer you right,' said Johnny. 'You'll soon figure the angles, you're not all that dumb.'

'Nice of you to say so.' Ossie smiled, but Johnny was not amused.

'Social director,' he said. 'That suit you?'

'What's in a name?' said Ossie.

'You get together with Bennie Munck and pick the acts you want for the floor show,' said Johnny. 'We don't want any trash. It's gotta come over good. Bennie knows the score.'

'Do I perform?' said Ossie.

'That's up to you,' said Johnny. 'You got a nice little act. Maybe you can slip it in now and then, but you won't have the time to run it as a regular item on the bills. I'll want to see you circulating, watching out for the big spenders coming in, and giving them a special hello so they start off feeling real good. That's mighty important in this line of business. That takes real acting, the way I see it.'

'Too true,' said Ossie.

Johnny poked a finger at Ossie. 'Get to know the guys who count around here. Pete Fallon will wise you up. Watch out for when you think maybe a bit of trouble might be blowing up. We don't like trouble here.'

'Who does?' said Ossie.

'Tact and plenty of savvy,' said Johnny. 'When the Law drops in we show them a nice time so we don't get any squawks.'

'I like that,' said Ossie.

'Bastards,' said Johnny without any emotion. 'All of them got their hands out. You'll soon pick up the business. Give it some tone.'

'I appreciate your confidence,' said Ossie. 'When do I start?'

'Finish up the week there.'

'What's going to happen to the others at the motel?' Ossie said. 'Charlie Stryker–'

–'and the broad,' said Johnny. He made a quick slicing movement with his hand. 'I'm hiring you. It's no package deal.'

'I just wondered,' said Ossie.

'Charlie Stryker's a good guy,' said Johnny. 'I might find something for him in town, but there's nothing for the broad.'

Ossie was about to point out that Olivia Halstedt was really no broad. He felt he owed her that much support at least.

But Johnny repeated that decisive slicing movement. 'I'm doing you a favour,' he said. 'Don't push me. We got all the broads we can use. You stuck on her or just shacking up?'

'She's been good to me,' said Ossie, and knew it didn't sound enough of an argument.

'That's what broads are for.' Johnny clicked on the inter-com. 'I want Vince,' he said.

Then he glanced again at Ossie. 'Plenty of chicks around here.'

'So I noticed,' said Ossie.

'Just don't let it get in the way of business,' said Johnny. 'I don't stand for that. When you get back to the motel I don't want to hear you been running off at the mouth. I don't like gabby guys. Check?'

Ossie nodded. This was the real Johnny Scimona speaking now, his dark eyes were hard and penetrating.

Ossie tried an ingratiating smile that would convince Johnny of his absolute integrity, but it slipped and left him just feeling foolish.

'I'm always discreet,' he said.

'That so?' said Johnny. 'You can do yourself a lot of good around here if you're smart. You can make the right contacts, mix with some real money – that's what you're after, same as anybody else, check?'

'Correct,' said Ossie. 'There's no substitute.'

'I won't do any shouting when I hear

you're creaming off a bit for yourself, you'll get plenty of offers – just okay them with me first.'

'That sounds like a very fair prospect,' said Ossie. He smiled but once more it raised no response from Johnny, just more of that hard searching look.

'You do anything out of line,' said Johnny flatly, 'you won't do it twice on account of you'll have a fatal headache.'

'That won't happen,' said Ossie.

As though to reinforce what had been flitting through Ossie's uneasy mind, Vince Flemmi stood in the doorway, sober suited as usual, a silent reminder of the calculated violence Johnny had at his command.

'That about ties it up,' said Johnny. 'If I want you again I'll send for you.'

'I am at your disposal,' said Ossie and knew he spoke the truth. It was too late now to refuse. That would surely be something Johnny Scimona would not allow.

Charlie Stryker didn't need to be told that there were going to be some changes at the motel, quite apart from Ossie's promotion.

'I figured it,' said Charlie. 'There was this bunch of guys poking around last week. One of Johnny's attorneys brought them, but I didn't get to be introduced, so I reckoned a deal was being cooked – and maybe I wouldn't be working here much longer.'

'It's possible,' said Ossie carefully. 'Life is in a state of flux, so I've always heard.'

'You've got one foot in the door already,' said Charlie. 'I never thought you'd last that long.'

'Neither did I,' said Ossie. 'Now I aim to cash in. I'll be right there in the middle of the heap – if you want money you have to be where money is.'

'They can be rough people,' said Charlie, 'and you're not one of them. Johnny Scimona finds a use for you, but that doesn't make you part of the Boston Family. When the chips are down the outsider has to lose.'

'That's a risk I'm prepared to take,' said Ossie. 'I'm after money, Charlie – big and quick.'

'That might turn out to be your epitaph, buddie boy,' said Charlie.

Although Ossie had told her nothing yet, Olivia guessed something was up. She had that sad questioning look in her eyes that he couldn't meet with any honesty; the mute reminder of all they had been to each other; the look of a woman who knows in her heart that she is going to lose.

Two nights before he was due to leave he tapped on the door of her cabin, as he had done so often. There was no answer and the door was locked and the cabin all dark. He had planned to tell her in the nicest possible way. They could always arrange to meet somewhere. Taper it off gently.

The next morning Charlie told him she had packed her bags and left in the early hours of the morning. He had no forwarding address and she had left no message for Oswald Trent, Esquire.

'You didn't expect any, did you?' said Charlie. 'She saved you the trouble of walking out on her.'

'That wasn't the way I wanted it,' said Ossie.

'That's the way you've got it.' There was a touch of the old acid in Charlie's tone. 'She knew there was no future in it for her. I reckon she showed some good sense, you had your fun so what are you beefing about?'

'No complaints,' said Ossie.

'Confidentially,' said Charlie, 'you are a bit of a louse.'

Ossie smiled and said he hoped to survive.

4

It took Ossie very little time to feel at home at the Club. He was the genial host to perfection – urbane and tactful and always beautifully turned out. He had the trained actor's retentive memory, and the regular big-spenders were flattered because he never forgot them once he had met them, and their women-folk just loved the discreet fuss he made over them, fixing their favourite tables and what they liked to drink and advising them about the menu. Attention like that made all the difference to an evening.

He was adaptable, and he had the sense not to pretend to the professional catering staff that he knew their work better than they did. Nothing can ruin a restaurant service faster than a disgruntled kitchen staff.

Ossie had the right manner, just enough deference to get on the right side of the men and women who did the work, especially the women. The result was that the general quality of the food and the service improved out of all recognition.

When he thought about it, he saw himself as a modern version of Beau Nash in Regency Bath. Except that what went on in the casino at the Carlton Country Club had nothing in common with the sedate play at Nash's Assembly Rooms.

Quite soon after Ossie had taken up his duties, there was rumble in the casino. A young man who had been losing heavily all night suddenly erupted. He lurched to his feet, heaved all the gear about, and declared that the goddam game was crooked – every goddam game in the place was crooked – and much more in the same vein.

There was some female screaming before the security boys nobbled the offender and whipped him out of sight through a side door. Ossie moved in and calmed the uproar as though he had been doing it all his life.

He apologised to the assembled ladies and gentlemen for the interruption, the young chap had obviously taken more liquor than he could hold, it was most regrettable, but one must make allowances for hot-headed youth, and so forth.

It was a beautiful performance. Classy. And so polite. Play was resumed with the minimum of delay.

Johnny Scimona had not been in the Club that night. The following morning he called Ossie into the office.

'You did a nice job,' he said. 'What I hear it went down okay. Angelo was running that table, he must be getting clumsy, letting a young punk like that cut wild, maybe he needs a vacation, maybe he's getting too old.'

Angelo, the croupier in question, was no older than Ossie. That was the last night he worked in the casino. And the bar was up against the young man who had caused all the fuss. He could lose his dollars someplace else.

The months slipped past, and Ossie fitted into his surroundings with remarkable ease. He let nothing disturb him, certainly not the knowledge that most of the men he was mixing with nightly were mobsters. The Carlton was a convenient meeting place for Johnny Scimona and his associates, where jobs were planned and policy discussed.

It would have been impossible for any observant man to spend his days and most of his nights in such a loaded atmosphere without picking up snippets of information, and Ossie was far more observant than average. He could put two and two together and come up with the right answer. Very little escaped him that might be worth knowing about. He developed the habit of being unobtrusively in the background when it counted, such as when the mob personalities were congregating for one of their business 'meets' which usually took place in a small private room that was strictly off-limits to the staff.

The social end of these meetings were Ossie's personal responsibility, and in this way he was able to assess the pecking order among the operators.

In the matter of 'respect' it became clear to him that Johnny Scimona was not quite at the top of the heap. He was big but not all that big.

For instance, the biggest slice of the money invested in the Carlton Country Club had come from Joey Rossi, and he was the man they all listened to when he gave an opinion.

He was lean and swarthily handsome, and still quite athletic in spite of his fifty years. Among the mob bosses he was the only one who made any regular use of the Club's facilities for exercise; he played a cunning game of tennis, rode better than most, and swam with vigour and style.

He had a law degree from Cornell, which helped when a piece of business looked like going off the rails too far. Unlike some of his associates he was never active in the casino, because he had too much regard for the importance of money to throw it around.

He kept his private life strictly private, and his wife Lucia was never at the Club. He had a country place in Connecticut, a model farm where his business partners were almost never invited to show themselves. He had also a place in Newport where he was more accessible. Lucia preferred to spend her time on the farm, and had nothing what-soever to do with her husband's business commitments. They had no children, and Joey was never known to show an interest in another woman, which was another personal item that marked him off from the rest.

He had travelled extensively outside the States, on business. There was little of the gambling set-up that he didn't know, in Antigua and Nassau and throughout the Caribbean; he had been one of the last operators to be eased out of Havana when Castro took over, and he had got his money out, which most of the others in the casino game had failed to do; it took more than a bearded *politico* in a khaki shirt to separate Joey Rossi from his loot. He still maintained excellent contacts in London, England.

There were few who could equal him when it came to 'laundering' the cash the mobs had collected so that the Federal sharks could get nothing out of their investigations. If you wanted to set up a fire-proof cheque fraud or a stock swindle you would consult Joey, for a fee; he didn't come cheap, but he was worth every dollar.

He seldom risked his own money, which is the safest way to make yourself into a rich man, and Joey now was well heeled.

He was astute and very cool in his dealings, and he would let others do the shouting. He could be quite charming when it suited him, but when a piece of action was going astray not even Johnny Scimona felt easy in his presence.

He didn't find it necessary to move around with a Vince Flemmi at his shoulder, but those who ought to know would tell you that the quickest way to leave this vale of tears was to run up against Joey on a serious business deal. And Joey never handled a gun himself; all he had to do was lift the phone and give the word.

Ossie knew exactly what he was about, and over an extended period he cultivated Joey Rossi without ever letting it become obvious.

He did it with much finesse, because he knew how the mob bosses regarded outsiders who got too ambitious, and he did not intend to finish up as part of the concrete foundations of a highway or a super-market.

He developed a special skill at being available when Joey wanted somebody to talk to who wasn't just another part of a mob outfit, somebody with a personality and a sense of humour and an amusing line of talk that didn't confine itself to hits and heists and rackets and 'whacking out' the opposition.

There were weeks on end when Joey wouldn't appear at the Carlton, and Ossie would hear that he was on one of his foreign trips, running some of the gambling 'junkets' that were proving so profitable, mostly to London and the Bahamas.

A group of fifty or so heavily loaded gamblers would be ferried across for a week of gambling at a selected casino; they would all have been checked as to their credit rating, and you had to be in a very good financial state to be accepted. The organiser would be paid around a hundred dollars a head by the casino operators, and would split the profits at the conclusion of the trip.

Since the gambling was done on credit, finance regulations were circumvented, and the final pay-out took place when the party returned to base, and with a man like Joey Rossi in charge nobody was ever going to welsh on what he owed. In fact, there were normally more applicants than vacancies on the trips.

Pete Fallon knew something about the business. 'You can't stop gamblers,' he said. 'Dump them down in plush surroundings and they go wild – broads and booze on the side, and the sharpest mechanics in the trade rigging the play. Take a feller like Joey Rossi, a reasonable trip for him would show a profit of eighty or a hundred grand. The Horizon Hotel in Antigua, that pays off one of the best, so does London, and there's never any shortage of suckers. If there were no suckers there wouldn't be any mobs.'

And Ossie had to agree that was the gospel truth. He himself was getting a comfortable living on the fringes of the mob. So far he had seen little violence, just an occasional drunken brawl on a busy Saturday night, expeditiously handled by the strong-arm boys before it got too serious. What might happen afterwards outside the Club area was no concern of the Club.

If one ignored the character and background of much of the clientèle, the Carlton had become nearly respectable. And Ossie felt he could take some of the credit.

In his private life he had not yet found a suitable successor to Olivia, nobody quite so convenient and amenable. He received plenty of social invitations, but he kept clear of wives and established girl friends who made it clear they would not kick him in the face if he made a proposition. He found a widow in Springfield, about his own age and with a small private income, with whom he conducted a very discreet liaison for some months.

There was nothing ecstatic about it for either of them, just a sensible arrangement which they both knew would be temporary. When the lady eventually took off to stay for an indefinite period with her sister in Chicago, Ossie knew the episode was over and was less than heartbroken. There would be another woman somewhere.

He had discovered the Boston restaurant that Joey Rossi favoured when he was spending any time in the city, and after a few abortive visits he just happened to stroll in one lunch time, and there was Joey sitting alone in a quiet corner.

Joey beckoned him over and invited him

to join him, and they shared an interesting meal. In due course the talk turned to London.

'It might be pleasant to go back there one day,' said Ossie.

'It's got something all of its own,' said Joey. 'Is there anybody there waiting to put a hand on you?'

Ossie smiled. 'If you mean am I wanted by the police, the answer is no. I'll go back when I've got enough cash to live the way I like.'

'It could happen,' said Joey, and dropped the subject.

Some days later Johnny Scimona called Ossie into the office.

'Joey's been talking to me about you,' he said. 'He's got an idea about you, and I gave him the go-ahead. You work for me, but I told him it was okay.'

The mob protocol had been observed. Ossie was Johnny's man until he gave him a release to work for somebody else. There would have been some compensation arranged between Johnny and Joey. A transfer fee.

Joey Rossi outlined the proposition. 'I want to have you along with me on my next London trip. I can arrange for the suckers to lose their money, that's no problem. But keeping them sweet, that's something else. You know London, the right places to go, the clubs and theatres and places that might be of interest. You could take care of the social scene, and every one would go on thinking they were having a hell of a good time.'

'And losing their money wouldn't hurt quite so much,' said Ossie.

'It's all in the mind,' said Joey. 'In the right atmosphere anything can happen. I've watched you handle the job here, and you're not operating on your own territory.'

'I wasn't exactly a star of the West End stage in London,' Ossie said.

'I know that,' said Joey. 'If you were Lord Olivier you wouldn't be working in a joint like this. But you still know your way around London.'

'I think so,' said Ossie.

'I select the suckers very carefully,' said Joey. 'There'll be plenty of pickings – a thousand dollars here and a thousand there, you wouldn't be insulted. Plus a bonus creamed off the top, and all expenses. You'd have to work for it, be on call all the time, fix this and fix that, steer them into the right places and see they don't get into too much trouble.'

'I get the picture,' said Ossie. 'It would need preliminary planning, and I've been away from London for a couple of years.'

'You'll go over there ahead of us,' said Joey. 'You'll get full backing all along the line, introductions, whatever you think you'll need. We don't skip anything.'

'Women?' said Ossie.

Joey shook his head. 'That will be taken care of, you won't have to involve yourself. There's no shortage of party girls over there.'

'There never was,' said Ossie.

'Refined ladies,' said Joey. 'No hookers in off the street.'

'Unthinkable,' said Ossie.

'I'll be running a group of about thirty this time,' said Joey. 'That's a handy number, not too difficult to keep tabs on them, and I'll supply you with a personal dossier on each of them so you'll know what to expect. Some of them have travelled with me before – there won't be any surprises.'

'No awkward bastards,' said Ossie.

'We think on the same lines,' said Joey. 'There won't be any publicity, we don't need any of that. It will just be a private trip for a bunch of sportmen who can afford the kind of money they'll be losing in luxurious surroundings and in the best of company.

Every item hand-picked. Including the operating staff.'

'I'm flattered,' said Ossie.

'Don't kid yourself,' said Joey pleasantly. 'It won't be any vacation.'

5

Joey Rossi was right. This first trip proved to be no rest cure for Ossie. He arrived in London a few days ahead of the main party to get some of the ground work done.

He was accommodated in a small furnished flat near Chester Square, and for the first time in his life he had considerable funds to draw on, which made it easy for him to keep away from the places where he might meet people who knew him in the bad old days. Like Doris, for instance. He supposed she was still technically his wife, although he hadn't heard anything about her for over two years. She wasn't listed in the London phone book, not even under her maiden name.

He was interested to meet some of Joey's

contacts, and it was gratifying to have them treat him as a man of importance; compared to Joey or Johnny Scimona they were nothing but amateurs; none of them ran a real organisation; London had nothing like the Boston Office operating. There was no co-ordination.

The only man who seemed to have anything going for him was Rufus Whittaker, an elderly type with a gentlemanly manner who made a fair living out of unloading items that the lesser fry found too hot to handle. Rufus was a character and very active for one of his advanced years.

Ossie found him a mine of information about certain aspects of the London scene. He would know, for example, who had lately done any business and what had been lifted and how much it might realise under the counter. If it was anything in the jewellery line it would probably have been offered to him, because he was something of an expert. Antiques and anything by one of the Old Masters he would never touch because they were too readily identified.

He had a prison record for fencing, and the police would call on him when there had been any action, but in recent years he had managed to keep himself clean without ever putting himself on the retired list. He lived alone in a cluttered apartment behind Victoria Station, and he was scared of drawing another prison sentence because he knew it would finish him.

Ossie thought he was better value than any of the others, and never threw him out when he turned up to pass the time of day.

Joey knew him and had some regard for him. 'If he was twenty years younger we might use him,' he said. 'There's no flies on the old boy.'

'He's still sharp,' said Ossie. 'He interests me. If I thought I might be spending much time here I might make a small investment in Rufus, as a sort of sleeping partner.'

'You'll be coming back,' said Joey.

The junket was going well. The party had been accommodated in very good hotels. The evenings and nights were full of action under the shaded lights, and money was being spent and lost in a highly satisfactory style – satisfactory to Joey and the casino bosses.

The regular casino sessions were the principal source of loot for the promoters, but there were also some spin-off activities that showed a handsome profit. For the sporting types who still had the stamina, a late party might be laid on in one of the hotel suites, with more inducements to lose your cash in convivial surroundings. There would be every drink you ever heard of, and some of those 'refined ladies' would be in attendance to do more than decorate the scene.

Nothing too outrageous would happen. No noisy orgy or public couplings on the carpet. The dice would roll and the booze would flow, and the bedrooms would be much in demand and the ladies would earn their considerable fees.

Ossie might be there from start to finish in the small hours, keeping a sober eye to see that nothing got really out of hand within the broadest of limits. He was the imperturbable Master of Ceremonies, and he did it without offending anybody, which was no small achievement since losers can get very touchy late at night.

He had arranged visiting membership facilities at some clubs where rich Americans were more than acceptable. He had made his number with a few of the most expensive restaurants of international repute, so that the customers on his private list would always find a table available. He discovered that the proprietors of some prestige establishments were willing to discuss the possibility of a kick-back in cash for business introduced, and he had not been insulted, as Joey had promised he wouldn't be. He was discovering in himself a slick facility in latching on to the perks that were coming his way, preferably in cash. It was a way of life all on its own, and cash was the yardstick.

No matter how late the session had been the night before, he contrived to be on the job bright and early in the morning. Joey thought he was a ball of fire and couldn't fault him on any of the incidentals that were keeping the trip sweet and smooth, and profitable.

If any of the clients felt like a dose of culture, Ossie had done his home-work and had worked up a snappy line of patter on the traditional items, such as Buckingham Palace, the Houses of Parliament, and Westminster Abbey. He made an interesting guide, he did the authentic English gentleman stuff, and he saw more of London than he had ever noticed before.

There was one memorable day when a pair

of super-rich Texans who had been regularly dropping large bundles of cash in the casino night after night insisted on his company in a hired Rolls for a lightning tour of the Cotswolds and Oxford and Stratford-on-Avon. It had been a break-neck excursion, and only the lack of time kept them away from Woburn Abbey and Blenheim. They were lavish spenders all through, and as a small token of their esteem they had presented Ossie with a platinum cigarette case.

He had very little time to himself, which was probably just as well, since he had more money in his pocket than ever before. He resisted the temptation to look up old friends who would recall him as a performer who had never quite made the grade, and he was not at all anxious to advertise his current employment.

In a plushy restaurant he did happen to meet a producer who knew him, but Ossie gave him no more than a distant nod and ushered his own party on to their reserved table and their preferential service, leaving the producer to wonder how the hell Oswald Trent had managed it because he had never amounted to much.

Joey and his associates were experts at 'skimming' the gambling take before any accounts were made up, and there was a heap of money being shovelled away under the counter before any tax officials got a look at it. That was how the real profits were being made, and hence the need for no publicity.

There were no headaches, just a smooth operation all the way, and when the final checking was done Ossie's slice came to over fifteen thousand dollars. He was more than happy with it, but Joey said it was just a start and the next time it would really jump.

When they ran a repeat performance Ossie already knew the drill, and he was able to organise himself better without having to rush hither and yon to set things up for the sportsmen with money to spend outside the casino. They had some boisterous spirits with them, and Ossie had to exercise some diplomacy about broken fixtures and furniture and complaints from residents in the neighbouring hotel suites. Far more tricky was the matter of a waitress on the late shift who claimed she had been indecently assaulted and then raped on the floor of a bathroom while a wild party was in progress next door so nobody heard her doing the screaming she insisted she had done. And she had the bruises to prove it in delicate places.

It was a fraught situation, because the character she pointed the finger at was the executive vice-president of a bank and a major stock holder in a number of ranking enterprises. He was a pillar of respectability, with a family of teenage daughters, and a socialite wife who would surely make the rest of his life hell if she ever got to hear of the episode.

Ossie had been at the party. He moved in smartly and took control with sober common-sense. He was so persuasive and sympathetic that he finally talked the girl into agreeing not to make a police matter of it. It took a substantial cash flow to mend her outraged virtue, and Ossie also came out of it nicely because the banker was a very grateful man and he showed it in the clearest fashion with a cheque that would never bounce. Ossie already had money on deposit in two London banks, and some items in a safe deposit, as insurance against the future.

Rufus Whittaker remained the only Londoner with whom he was happy to spend any of his limited free time. Joey himself approved of the association because Rufus didn't try to horn in on anything and cut himself a slice, not like some of the other London operators who reckoned they might be in Joey's class when Joey wouldn't even give them the time of day.

The old guy had some character, and he still knew his way around. One day they might want to unload something privately in London, and Rufus might just be the guy to handle it. He was safe and he wouldn't pull any fast ones.

When the final accounting was done, Ossie collected just a little over forty thousand dollars from all sources, and life was looking very rosy indeed.

He was thus more than a shade disappointed when he found that Joey was leaving him out of the next trip.

'There'll be no scope for you this time,' said Joey. 'I'm giving London a miss for a while – too many hits close together is never good for business, it gets the revenue boys too interested in us. I'm taking a small party to Paradise Island to work the Lucayan Bay Casino. The Miami family own the place and they're not the best people to deal with – they'll squeeze me if they get half a chance.

Dino Collenti runs it, the real boss is Jackie Nene and his idea of a square deal is sixty-forty the right way up for him. And you have to sweat blood to get it out of him. There's nothing there but the beach and the casino – no pickings for you this time. It's only a small party and I don't plan to spend more than four or five days there. So I can't cut you in, but I'm lining up a big one for Caracas later with a really big pay-off. This Lucayan Bay thing is something I want to pull off – it's personal. The Miami mob don't let any outsiders run the casino or bring over any parties except on their conditions, and they've been known to react pretty roughly in the past. A lot of people around here don't think I can make a deal, they reckon Jackie Nene will have me skinned before I leave with any loot. I aim to prove them wrong. I can handle Jackie Nene.'

'I'm sure you can,' said Ossie.

They were both wrong. The day before Joey was expected back from Paradise Island the news filtered through to Johnny Scimona some hours before it was made public. Joey Rossi's body had been picked up by a fishing boat off Great Stirrup Cay with a hole in the back of his head that had not been made by any marlin or tarpon.

The Boston Office mobilised immediately and Ossie heard about it only at second hand because he wasn't in the family. Joey Rossi's death had to be paid for and with interest, or the Boston mob would cease to be of any account.

Jackie Nene was hard to get at, but two of his closest associates met very messy ends – an exploding car killed one outside his own front door, and the other was found with his head jammed in the wash-basin in the toilet at a motel and a bullet through his neck.

The mob war was under way, and its ramifications spread as the weeks went by. Jackie Nene was known to have brought in some hit-men from outside, professional assassins who worked in pairs and for a price.

Vince Flemmi was ambushed one night as he drove out of the Carlton Country Club alone in Johnny Scimona's car. Johnny should have been in the car, but he had decided to spend the night at the Club in the company of a new young woman who had just joined the team, and who was credited with some interesting tricks, which saved Johnny's life.

Vince Flemmi fought a running battle for a hundred yards before they got him and blasted most of his head off and then set fire to the car.

The following evening there was an incident at a café attached to a motel in Quincy, Massachusetts, that was used as a meeting place by some of the Boston mob. A pair of hooded gunmen appeared in the doorway, sprayed the place with shot-guns, and took off in a car that had been waiting outside. The business took a matter of seconds, and the mess was considerable.

There were two fatal casualties, both middle-aged men who had no kind of connection with any mob but who had the bad luck to be in the wrong place at the wrong time. A young girl was blinded, and several other peaceful citizens received injuries that would disfigure them for life.

None of the Boston boys got in the way of the barrage. They were on the floor and under the table as soon as those shot-guns came into view.

The heat was distinctly on all round. It was the first serious mob war since 1969. Bodies were being found here and there, all of them identified as mob killings – and most of them were. The bullet through the back of the head was the mob label. Quite a few operators on both sides went missing and were never found. They would be in the river or mixed up with the concrete somewhere.

Johnny Scimona had decided it was prudent to 'hit the mattress' and hide out somewhere private. Public opinion and Press editorials were demanding action, and Police Commissioners in the troubled areas were making life difficult.

Ossie knew his own position was tricky. He wasn't in the Boston mob, only on the fringes as an employee. But he didn't think that would impress the police – or those gunmen up from Miami.

It had been good while it lasted, with the cash flowing in, now it was all falling apart. He was in a Boston hotel and he was not at all anxious to stir abroad because his name might be on some hit-man's list.

After he had been sweating in isolation for a week or so, Johnny Scimona reached him on the phone.

'I don't like this one little bit,' said Ossie.

'Who does?' said Johnny. 'It's mattress time so we all lose money, nobody is out pushing any business on account of nobody knows who gets blasted next. But we don't back down. Joey Rossi wouldn't like that.

Nobody pushes us around. We got muscles. You nervous?'

'Very,' said Ossie. 'It's not my kind of thing.'

'Okay,' said Johnny abruptly. 'Take a trip.'

'I've been thinking of that,' said Ossie.

'Don't sit around,' said Johnny. 'It might get too rough for you … been nice knowing you.'

Ossie had been about to explain that he happened to be holding some items for Joey Rossi. Stocks and bonds worth a real packet. Genuine. Nothing forged or hot.

But Johnny had cleared the line and he hadn't given Ossie a number. Ossie thought about the problem, but not for long. Joey was dead and the mob was busy fighting for its continued existence. And the bonds were money. Big money.

When he fetched up in London a few days later, Oswald Trent was a man of substance. In recent years Rufus Whittaker had been handicapped by lack of working capital, and Ossie was now in the position to supply that. The two of them were in step, and Ossie was very ready to learn all he could from the old pro.

They made an effective partnership. Rufus

had the good-will and the contacts, and with Ossie's money behind them they were able to extend their activities. The story had got about that Ossie had been a ranking member of the Mafia in the States, which made the more ambitious operators all the more anxious to do business with him. The prestige was worth money.

In a matter of months Rufus had become no more than a sleeping partner, which suited him since his health had begun to fail. He moved to a flat in Brighton to enjoy the bracing sea air, and Ossie visited him once a week to run over their current transactions.

By this time Ossie knew nearly as much about 'hot' jewellery as Rufus did, and he had introduced a new line that was proving very profitable – dealing in stolen money that was too easily identified for gangs to handle. Ossie paid a percentage, seldom more than twenty, and moved the notes eventually through their Continental associates.

It was a busy life, and he was always on the move since he did not intend to risk coming under police observation. It was his deliberate policy not to be too accessible, and if you had something special to get rid of he might agree to meet you, but only when and where he chose.

Rufus caught a bad dose of bronchitis, and died in a nursing home very tidily and without fuss. He had made a will which named Oswald Trent as his sole heir, and Ossie gave him a very dignified funeral.

The London papers gave little space to the mob war in the States, and Ossie had no other way of getting any news from over there. From the very occasional items he chanced to see it appeared that the war still went on sporadically, flaring up now and then when it was thought to be over. There would have to be some kind of a truce eventually before the mobs ruined each other. It had happened before. And it would happen again.

One of the Sunday coloured supplements ran a feature on the long series of killings to illustrate the many hazards of life in the USA, along with Black Power activists and the campus rioters, and similar pressure groups.

Ossie recognised some of the names of men he had met at the Carlton Country Club, and he knew he had got out just in time.

Johnny Scimona had told him to take a

trip, and Johnny was probably dead by now.

So there was nothing and nobody to connect him with the Boston Office. He had used his head, and he hadn't come away with empty pockets either, which proved at least to himself that he was smart enough. Not many outsiders had the nerve to get money out of the mob.

For a while he had felt a secret uneasiness about the stuff he had been holding for Joey Rossi. Joey said a man named Mattie would be calling from Providence to collect the bonds, but he hadn't arrived. Ossie had waited as long as he dared, but he didn't know anybody it might be safe to contact.

He had done the obvious thing, and those stocks and bonds had long since been converted into cash and added to his working capital.

He was in the clear, and he was making money. His private life was also again in a better shape. Laura Heydon was a smart and attractive woman in the middle thirties who was earning a very good living in a large magazine group. All around her she had seen marriages flop, and she made it clear to any male who might show interest that marriage didn't figure in her own planned future.

She would deny that she was promiscuous, but if she took a fancy to a man something was likely to happen to their mutual comfort. And when it was over it was over.

She was, she considered, a healthy and well-adjusted woman in the prime of life. And to go with her handsome salary she had a very pleasant flat near Lords cricket ground.

She met Ossie at a party where they were both being rather bored. She guessed he was a bit of a rogue, but he was amusing and quite presentable; they had dinner together, and he didn't bore her with a lot of bogus talk about his business and how important he was. He didn't talk business at all, which made a pleasant change from the escorts she had been lumbered with recently.

They both knew how that first evening would end, and it did. They went very well together and no harm was done to anybody.

Ossie didn't move in with her because she wouldn't have that, but he slept with her three or four nights a week, and they went out together whenever the opportunity arose. It was a mature and very satisfactory relationship, and like a sensible woman with few illusions Laura accepted the fact that there would be many occasions when she couldn't contact him because he didn't know for sure where he would be. She didn't press him for details, she was no frustrated spinster in search of a husband and security.

She was very happy with the way her life was going, and she didn't feel she had to pry into his business affairs, whatever they might be. They were both working on a short lease, and they both knew it.

Ossie had been around, but he could still turn on the charm and make her feel right out of this world. He knew the right places to take a girl, and he was never short of money.

He might be some kind of a gentlemanly crook, but that had nothing to do with her. He looked all right, he knew how to behave, he was amusing to be with, and he never bored her.

He brought her flowers and occasionally little items of quite expensive jewellery, and he never omitted to tell her how marvellous and exciting she was when she was allowing him the freedom and co-operation of her agile body.

As a lover she rated him pretty highly, and

Laura's standards were exacting. She might even have some regrets when the time came for them to separate.

PART TWO

6

Sam Harris had an unusual problem. In normal circumstances he would have accepted it as a bonus beyond his craziest dreams to have the guarantee of three square meals a day and the freedom of a lady's bed without having to fork over any cash at all.

The obliging lady in question was his landlady, Lily, and although she was admittedly no raver and on the wrong side of fifty, she could still raise a satisfactory gallop after a couple of gins and she was not all that painful to look at either.

It should have been gilt-edged for Sam. All home comforts and no overheads.

But there were snags, of course, because Lily knew enough about Sam's recent activities to make life more than awkward for him, so he just had to keep her sweet.

It had all come about as the result of an abortive attempt to raid the safe at 'Bernie's Place', a prosperous social club in the Home Counties. This enterprise was well outside Sam's professional range, and he had talked Percy Cater into doing the important job on the safe. Percy was an expert safe-blower; he was also a lodger at Lily's place with Sam.

There had been a third accomplice who had supplied the inside information and who was to take care of the alarm system. Freddie Stainer worked at the club and had been promised a slice of the loot. He was not meant to be on the premises when the safe was blown, but he had very good reason not to trust the other two, and he suspected, quite rightly, that they intended to diddle him out of his share.

Accordingly, after Percy Cater had got the safe open and Sam was helping him to gather up the cash, Freddie Stainer appeared, with a gun in his hand. He said he was going to scoop the lot, and in the fracas that followed Percy Cater got himself shot dead.

Sam took off for the open spaces, as was his custom when the situation got too fraught, with Freddie Stainer after him. In the course of his hurried exit Sam ran over Freddie Stainer, and only later did he learn that Stainer's injuries had proved fatal.

So Sam went into hiding, with a little cash in his pocket, hoping not to be officially connected with the unfortunate business.

Very few people could link him with the dead Percy Cater – but Lily was one of them. So far Percy had not been identified.

Sam's luck did not hold good, and it was through his own fault eventually. He unwisely got himself involved in a blackmail job that was right out of his reach, and it left him without his car and stripped of his loose cash.

Hoping that Lily still knew nothing of what he had been up to, he headed back to take refuge with her. He then discovered that he was too late to retreat – Percy Cater had been identified and Lily had seen it in the paper.

The reality of the situation was made clear to Sam the very first night he was back in Lily's bedroom. She was prepared to forget her duty as a law-abiding citizen – she would make no visit to the police to inform them that she knew who had been with Percy Cater and Freddie Stainer inside 'Bernie's Place'. She said she was even willing to accept Sam's version of what had happened, and he had told her very nearly the truth.

The tender trap had closed about him, and he was safe as long as true love endured, and he continued to render satisfaction.

Lily owned the house, she had a divorce behind her, and some investments that brought in a handy income. Sam had begun sleeping with her soon after he moved in with her, and he had managed to reawaken in her an appetite for sex that had been dormant for too long, and now she had him where she wanted him.

Sam was in the middle forties, also divorced; sharp and smartly dressed, he avoided regular work and lived on his wits, scratching here and there, always with an eye open for the big thing that could come along one day. An optimistic small-time operator, he had a glib tongue and a weakness for the kind of bird who would never give him the time of day, normally.

He had wavy ginger hair that he was inordinately proud of, and a neat fair moustache. Even when insolvent, which was not seldom, he contrived to look prosperous, and if you listened to him long enough you would get the impression that he had a heap of good things going for him, which was never truly the case.

An unlovable rogue, out for Number One, that was Sam Harris.

Even before the fiasco at 'Bernie's Place' Lily had been dropping hints about what she had in mind for the two of them. She was really a respectable woman, and she had reached the age when a woman expects to have the company of a spouse against the dreaded onset of age, and so forth.

Sam had been well aware that the danger signals were being hoisted, and the tinkle of wedding bells were no part of his plans for the future. Not with Lily. She was okay for a convenient piece of fun on a temporary basis, but if she thought she was going to stick a permanent label on him she was right off her nut.

There had to be somebody younger, maybe with a bit of real cash, just waiting somewhere for Sam to stride into her life. In spite of many rebuffs at the hands of birds with spending money, Sam cherished the dream that he had to get lucky one fine day.

In fact, when he had left Percy Cater to do that disastrous thing at the club he had finished with Lily, although she didn't know it since she had been out of the house at the time. She had served her purpose.

It was indeed lucky for Sam that he was able to slide back under cover with Lily and talk her out of suspecting that he had ever thought of abandoning her, and without a fond farewell.

He had a safe refuge, but the price was

going to be high. Lily wasn't hinting any longer. She put the case with no finesse at all: as his wife she couldn't be made to tell the police what she knew about him, could she? There was also the fact that she had become ever so fond of him.

Sam had seen this crisis coming. He assured her very sincerely that he would be proud and happy to make her Mrs Harris in due course when things had settled down a bit. In a further flight of fancy he even undertook to look for a nice respectable job with a steady income, a notion which would have paralysed most of the characters who knew Sam.

'You wouldn't like it if I lived off you, baby,' said Sam gravely. 'I mean, I got my self-respect–'

'–And it does you credit, Sammie,' said Lily fondly, ignoring the fact that Sam hadn't put his hand in his pocket for their household expenses for some time. 'But we won't have to wait too long, will we? After all, it doesn't have to concern anybody but you and me, and we aren't exactly a pair of kids, are we?'

Too bloody true.

'That nasty business about Percy Cater, that'll soon blow over and be forgotten about, it isn't even in the papers any more,'

Lily went on, 'and they can't prove you were there, they don't know your name or anything–'

But you know, and you can drop me right in the dirt any time you feel like it. A hell of a basis for married life.

Sam persuaded her that it would be safer for him to remain under cover for a few weeks, and she liked that because it increased her complete control of the situation. When Sam eventually felt he couldn't stand the incarceration any longer, Lily went with him, late in the evening, her arm linked snugly in his, full of domestic chat and togetherness.

Sam began to have twinges of desperation. The affair at 'Bernie's Place' was being no longer mentioned in the press. There had been another motorway murder-rape. A London suburban bank had been held up by a mob of armed raiders who had got away with over two hundred thousand pounds after shooting up some of the staff, one lady cashier having most of her face blown off. There had been a fashionable version of a gang-bang in a luxury flat near Grosvenor Square which was causing some embarrassment to the parents of the participants since the girl involved was insisting on naming names.

Miscellaneous explosions had continued to happen here and there in our peaceful cities, and the police forces throughout the land had more than they could hope to cope with.

It was going to be all right for Sam. Lily was now the problem. There had to be some safe way of getting clear of her without risking himself, like having to marry her.

It was Lily's custom once a week to spend an evening visiting her married sister, Ethel, who lived in Kingston. Ethel was a couple of years older than Lily, and her husband, Harry, ran a moderately successful iron-mongery business; Sam had met the pair of them, once only, and that had been enough for him.

He had found Harry as thick as two planks, and Ethel, a sharp-nosed suspicious old cow had given him a frosty reception from the start; she had guessed that he was no ordinary lodger – Lily had that glow about her, and Ethel could sniff illicit sex.

Sam was thus reluctant to let himself be paraded as Lily's fiancé, and he coaxed Lily into resuming her visits to Kingston on her own, which allowed him some regular and welcome periods of liberty. He had to get back into circulation, and he still had a little cash available, which he was prudently keeping to himself. It would have been a lot more if the job at 'Bernie's Place' had come off.

However, it suited Sam to let Lily think he was really skint; it helped her to imagine that she had him right under her control. Whenever she slipped him a fiver he made a big business of noting it all down for future repayment, and Lily was by now so besotted that she convinced herself that he was a man with character and genuine principles who only needed the loving support of a good woman, such as herself, to turn him into an upright citizen. It was rough on his nerves, but Sam fostered this delusion, and continued to look for some kind of an escape route.

Early one evening, he was out on one of his solo excursions, looking over some of his old haunts, checking who was about and what might be going on; it was time he got himself hooked into something with a payday on the end of it. He was sitting in a Chiswick pub near the river and not doing himself much good because there was a lamentable dearth of talent.

He was about to move on when he saw

through the window a bird parking a car in a hurry, and as soon as she got out he knew her.

It was Carrie Newland, and she didn't even wait to lock her little blue Fiat before she turned into the pub. She wore a red trouser suit with a frilly cream blouse and her figure was still just right for the outfit. She was tall and willowy, not beautiful, but striking enough to be worth watching as she stood in the doorway, smoothing her long dark hair and checking over the bar. Sexy and tough.

Sam was remembering about her husband, Tommy, and where he was. A couple of years back Sam and Carrie had been closer friends than Tommy Newland would have liked if he had known. It had been a tricky business, and although Carrie had been terrific in bed Sam had begun to sweat about Tommy finding out. There were few things Sam liked less than being beaten to a pulp by an irate husband, and Tommy had a nasty reputation.

So Sam, true to form, had manufactured excuses and slid off.

It was different now. Tommy Newland was in the first months of an enforced official vacation and under maximum security after a spectacular piece of breaking-and-entering which had made front page news. And here was Carrie all on her own.

Sam intercepted her smartly before she had reached the bar, and the look she gave him was not all that frosty.

'Evening, Carrie,' he said. 'Nice to see you again.'

'Sam,' she said, 'Sam Harris,' and from the way she said it she might have been almost pleased to meet him.

'Nobody else,' said Sam. 'You look a real knock-out, if I may say so.'

'Fancy talk,' she said. 'I could never stop you, Sammie. Just a talker.'

Sam grinned because they both knew different. 'What are you drinking? Vodka and lime, same as usual?'

'Still the old smoothie,' she said, not displeased. 'Okay, make it a big one.'

'You know me,' said Sam, saucy. 'Never less than big.'

'Dirty talk now,' said Carrie and flashed her strong white teeth. 'Not the time or the place, Sammie.'

Carrying her drink, he followed her across to his table by the window, catching her perfume and watching the provocative little movement of her neat hips. He was remembering quite vividly the way she looked without her clothes. Pretty good all round. She was thirty four and in excellent running order.

They settled themselves. 'Well, Carrie,' said Sam brightly, 'you are a sight for sore eyes and you can quote me on that.'

'If I didn't know you better,' she said, 'you might be good for my morale.'

'Very harsh,' he said, shaking his head. 'I could never forget you, Carrie. It was just that circumstances were against me.'

'You were scared of Tommy,' she said.

He patted her thigh. 'I didn't want to make any trouble for you.'

She laughed and drank some of the vodka. 'You don't know the half of it. Incidentally, Sam Harris, if you're after what I know damn well you're after I'm not in the mood.'

He squeezed her leg and then removed his hand. 'I was sorry to hear about Tommy. That was lousy luck, getting picked up like that.'

She shrugged, the corners of her mouth turned down. 'It happened.'

'Proper lousy luck,' Sam repeated. 'Is he coping okay inside?'

'What do you think?' she said.

'Rough,' said Sam, 'for a feller with his talent. He pulled off some nice smooth jobs in his time. Tommy had style and imagination.'

'We must get you to write him a testimonial,' she said. 'Say four years from now.'

'I mean it,' said Sam. 'I couldn't believe it when I heard what happened.'

'Perhaps he had it coming to him,' she said.

Sam stared at her. 'But he must have left you fixed okay. You can't blame Tommy if he came unstuck.'

'I can blame Tommy for plenty of things,' she said.

'I seem to remember reading that they never found the gear,' said Sam.

Carrie met his gaze. 'He didn't leave it with me,' she said.

'Fifty thousand quids' worth,' said Sam. 'And they never got a sniff at it.'

'Neither did I,' she said. 'I had the fuzz tailing me for weeks, they turned the flat inside out, it was hell, and they wouldn't believe that I wasn't even in London when he did it.'

Sam darted an anxious look around the bar. A couple of men had come in since Carrie had arrived; from the greeting they had received from the barman they were evidently regulars; Sam normally reckoned he could spot the plain clothes fuzz – there was something about the quick way they checked a place over as soon as they came in.

'It's all right,' said Carrie softly, 'don't get yourself in an uproar, they've been leaving me alone the last few weeks, nobody tailed me here – have they got you on the wanted list, Sammie?'

'Me?' said Sam. 'They can't touch me.'

'That makes a change,' she said wryly. 'What have you been up to since I saw you last?'

'Nothing to worry about. Things have been very quiet. But I'm not short, I can manage. You still at the same pad?'

'I moved out before Tommy got sent up,' she said. 'We split up. Things sort of fell apart, what with one thing and another, and we agreed to separate. I've been living on my own, and that's something else the fuzz didn't want to believe.'

'Living on your own? That's a laugh. When you came in here you were looking for somebody,' said Sam. 'You don't drink on your own in a pub, not you.'

'Well I wasn't looking for you,' she said, 'so don't kid yourself.'

'That doesn't sound friendly,' he said.

'You walked out on me.'

'My mistake,' said Sam. 'You looking for anybody I know?'

'I could tolerate another drink,' she said, 'and don't imagine it'll buy you anything more than a few minutes of my time.'

'I'm the sporting type,' said Sam. 'I'll gamble.'

He got up and went across to the bar. The two characters who had aroused his interest had finished their pints and were leaving with a third party. So all was well. And the idea of Carrie living on her own had attractive possibilities. It had to be a feller she was looking for, which meant there might be some competition.

Maybe he wouldn't turn up.

When he rejoined Carrie she said, 'Have you ever heard of Ossie Trent?'

'I've heard of him,' said Sam.

'I was hoping to meet him here,' she said.

'I hope he fell down a drain,' said Sam, 'then I can take you out to dinner, for old time's sake.'

'Sentimental Sam Harris in a pig's eye,' she said sweetly. 'You're no use to me. I have to find Ossie Trent and you wouldn't be any help.'

'I know his reputation,' said Sam. 'He wouldn't stay long in his line of business if he could be contacted too easily. He handles only high class merchandise.'

'I know all that,' she said. 'Tommy was my husband and I'm not stupid, Sammie.'

'You're trying to flog him something,' he said.

Carrie smiled. 'I don't have to tell you anything.'

'I can still add up,' said Sam. 'Given a little time and the right kind of inducement I might be able to put you in touch with Oswald Trent, esquire.'

'Inducement, Sammie?' The curve of her mouth was inviting. 'Whatever can you have in mind?'

'It'll keep,' he told her. 'You're not going to tell me what this is all about, are you?'

She just dipped her head on one side and gave him more of the smile.

'You don't trust me,' said Sam.

'Give me one good reason why I should,' she said. 'I didn't invite you in this time, Sammie. I know you and I know your limitations. There's nothing in this for you.'

'I'm making you a genuine offer, I don't have anything too urgent on my plate just now, so I'm ready to pitch in and see what I can do.'

'Applause, applause,' she said.

'Okay,' said Sam. 'Have a good laugh. But just suppose I happen to locate this Ossie Trent, what do I tell him?'

'Nothing.'

She delved into her bag, took out a pocket diary, tore off a page and wrote down a phone number and passed it to him.

'Tell him nothing. Just call me. Will you do that, Sammie?'

'I never could resist a lady in distress,' he said.

'Still the same old smoothie,' she said. She finished her drink quickly and stood up. 'Now I have to be off. Perhaps I'll be hearing from you soon?'

'Could be,' said Sam. 'How about that cosy little dinner with soft lights and all that?'

'Next time, if you turn up anything good.' She switched on the bedroom smile. 'There's nothing like an old friend in an emergency, is there?'

'Not so old,' he said. 'I can prove it any time you like.'

She fluttered her fingers at him in farewell and walked prettily out of the bar. Through the window he watched her slide herself neatly into that little Fiat, and then she was away, leaving Sam with some interesting speculations.

This had to be some unfinished business concerning Tommy Newland, and there might be a profit in it somewhere. With Carrie as a bit of a bonus? Why not?

7

Lily did not return home that night, which did not worry Sam unduly. He had been out late himself, making the preliminary moves that just might bring him up alongside Ossie Trent in the end; circulating and prodding and listening, and testing the general temperature.

The initial snag was that Ossie Trent's line of business was too high-class for Sam and most of his contacts, and reliable information was thus hard to come by. Ossie was highly elusive unless you were on his list and in good odour and of sound professional repute. Sam knew he had a chore ahead of him, and he was going to need liberty of movement.

So Lily was going to be the problem he was nowhere near solving. He guessed she had decided to spend the night with her sister in Kingston; she had probably tried to ring him while he was out, and she would want to know just what he had been doing until close on midnight. It was just like being married to her.

However, it was a relief to sleep on his own for a change, and he had plenty on his mind.

He had re-established contact with Carrie, and Tommy Newland was securely tucked away for a number of years. Tommy was admitted by the experts to be a jewel thief of particular talent and resource who visited only the very best addresses, and after painstaking research. In fact, to have your residence done over by Tommy was an excellent proof that your wife's trinkets were the real thing, and he never left any mess behind.

He chose his jobs with care and carried them out with speed and finesse, and he seldom needed to operate more than once or twice a season.

Before he fell asleep that night Sam spent a long time trying to recall the exact details of Tommy Newland's one and only foul-up which had put him behind bars. Carrie would know, and he'd coax it out of her. It was all tied up with her search for Ossie Trent, it had to be.

He had just finished shaving the next morning when he heard the key in the front door. He went out to the landing to greet Lily, and a very sour face glared up the stairs at him. It belonged to Ethel, Lily's sister from Kingston.

'You're still here then,' she snapped. 'Get yourself dressed and come down here.'

'Where's Lily?' he asked mildly. The old crow was all steamed up about something.

'Get dressed and I'll tell you. Make yourself look respectable, and hurry up.' Ethel banged into the living-room.

Sam was in his shirt sleeves. Anybody would think he had presented himself starkers. He withdrew to his own bedroom, which he did not normally occupy; he put on a tie and his jacket and his shoes, brushed his crinky hair, and assured himself he looked as respectable as a bank manager at least. Then he popped down the stairs.

Ethel stood in the middle of the room, her eyes stony and as full of open hostility as ever; her mouth was a tight mean line.

'You'll have to be moving out,' she said tartly. 'You can't stay here any longer. You understand that? You're leaving, now.'

'Hold it,' said Sam. 'Lily might have something to say about that. I'll hear it from her first.'

'She's dead,' said Ethel. 'She got run over in the road last night, she died in the hospital early this morning–'

–'I'm sorry,' said Sam, and he was genuinely shaken at the news.

'No doubt you are.' Ethel sniffed and folded her arms across her bosom. 'She never recovered consciousness. It was the driver's fault and we are going to sue, naturally. My husband will see to that. It was a lorry.'

'What a bloody awful thing,' Sam whispered, mostly to himself. Poor old Lily. He dropped into a chair and lit a cigarette, and when he glanced up at Ethel he could find no sign that she had been crying.

'There's no need to swear,' she said. 'That won't improve things.'

'You're a heartless old bag,' he said.

'I know all about you,' she said, 'and I won't have you in this house any longer. It just suited you, living here and sponging on my sister – she was too soft and trusting for her own good. I know all about your sort so you can just pack your traps and be off with you.'

Sam pulled at his cigarette. For one nasty moment he had thought Lily had told her sister about the business at 'Bernie's Place'

– which case Ethel would probably have arrived with a flock of coppers.

'I had my suspicions about you the first time I set eyes on you,' Ethel went on. 'I warned Lily, I told her you were no good–'

–'She wanted to marry me,' said Sam placidly.

Ethel glared and swallowed noisily. 'I thought as much. She must have been out of her mind. A man like you couldn't make her happy.'

'I wasn't doing so badly,' said Sam.

Ethel made an abrupt gesture of dismissal. 'We'll be putting the house up for sale.'

'I don't mind keeping an eye on it for a while,' said Sam. 'As a favour to the family. It takes time to sell a house, and I wouldn't mind stopping on for a bit.'

'You've got your nerve,' said Ethel. 'You'd have the place stripped in no time, and I'll tell you something else – when you leave here you won't take anything that doesn't belong to you, I'll make sure of that. I'm the only next-of-kin, and it all comes to me, so the sooner you clear out the better.'

Sam stood up and stretched. 'As I said before, you're a right old bag. Suppose I tell you Lily made a will and left it all to me?'

'You're a liar,' said Ethel promptly. 'She

wasn't that daft. My husband will be along in a minute with the van and he won't want to find you still here.'

'You don't waste much time,' said Sam. 'Hell, turning up with a van already and she only died a few hours ago.'

'I know what should be here,' said Ethel. 'So don't you try any sneaky tricks.'

'It beats me how a nice woman like Lily had a bitch of a sister like you,' said Sam.

'My Harry will see to you when he gets here,' said Ethel venomously.

'Now you got me really scared,' said Sam.

Ethel swept out of the room, and presently he could hear her thumping around upstairs, probably checking that he hadn't already nicked any of the furniture. There hadn't been a word of regret from her about Lily's abrupt and tragic ending, flattened under a lorry. Even Sam didn't like to think about it – he had wanted his problem solved, but not like that. Now he was free to leave, which was what he had been looking for.

Tossed out into the street, and by a vicious old crow.

It had been Lily's habit to cash a cheque once a month to cover the house-keeping and incidental expenses; she had this old-fashioned belief in paying cash, a belief which

Sam was very far from sharing with her.

He knew where she kept the cash, in a drawer in her desk, and he also knew where she kept the key.

Ethel was still slamming around up there. Sam stroked his nose and decided that this was a bit of Lily's property that wouldn't find its way into Ethel's claw.

Sixty odd quid, most of it in fives. He folded them away inside his pocket, and he also took Lily's little personal account book. So now Ethel couldn't prove a thing – and she wouldn't have the nerve to try to search him before he left.

There were some bits and pieces in his room, most of his gear he had taken with him when he set out on the job at 'Bernie's Place' since he didn't intend to return.

One small case would take the lot, and Ethel stood there by the bed and watched him pack; shirts and socks and so forth.

'Satisfied?' Sam gave her a saucy grin as he closed the case. 'I haven't nicked any of the family heirlooms, and there isn't room in there for a carpet, honest, lady.'

She stuck out her hand. 'You have a key,' she said. 'I want it. You're not leaving here with a key to the front door.'

'Anybody would think I was a burglar,'

said Sam.

'I wouldn't put it past you,' she snapped.

Sam dug in his pocket and produced the key. She followed close behind him down the stairs. He halted at the front door.

'What about the funeral?' he said. 'I'd like to be there–'

–'Don't bother, you won't be expected. In fact, you wouldn't be welcome.'

'If I wasn't a gentleman I'd tell you what you can do with yourself,' said Sam, and let himself out. He remembered to slam the door behind him. End of episode.

Before the morning was over he had found a furnished room with partial board in a place on the Maida Vale edge of Kilburn; nothing special, but convenient and very few questions asked. His new landlady was no Lily. She was heavily pregnant and she lived with a muscular character in the basement who came up and handled the cash in advance without the formality of an introduction. So Sam had to part with a large slice of what he had lifted from Lily's desk.

He sat in a coffee house near the Marble Arch and began to do a preliminary study in the matter of Ossie Trent. He tried a selection of phone numbers without getting anything. Most of those he spoke to were reluctant to admit they knew anything about Ossie Trent, and that was probably because they didn't trust Sam owing to his well-known habit of looking out strictly for himself if and when trouble looked likely, a habit that does not encourage co-operation or create any goodwill.

There was also the drawback that Sam was moving out of his class, which in itself does not make for quick results. So it was proving negative for quite a while.

However, although he might be short of the qualities that build a sterling character, Sam had more than his share of persistence, and in spite of rebuffs and personal insults he kept digging away, confident that he would unearth somebody who would give him a lead.

Albert Raikes was a knowledgeable little man, with silvery grey hair and a quiet taste in clothes. He had a flat in a modern block near Baker Street, where he lived in a comfortable and unobtrusive style. He had no ascertainable occupation, and let it be understood that his investments took care of his needs, and made it possible for him to travel very frequently. He had created the image of a middle-aged gentleman of independent means, respectable and conservative, and perhaps a little dull.

A widower now for some years, he periodically availed himself of the expensive services of a discreet one-time actress who was no longer in the first flush of youth and who had not quite made the grade on stage or screen. Her clientèle were select and regular, and her entertainment was conducted with the utmost decorum. No whips or kinky gear, just straight sex, preferably in the afternoon and by appointment. A tidy arrangement that suited Albert Raikes who liked to have all aspects of his life under his own control.

But there was more to him than any of his neighbours ever suspected. There were a few characters who knew him as a man who might be interested in supplying the working capital for an enterprise if the conditions satisfied him: the job had to be fool-proof, the operators had to be the best in the business and personally known to him, and the cut would be sixty/forty in Bertie's favour.

From his cosy flat he maintained a wide range of acquaintances, and he was ready to pay spot cash for information that might result in a business deal. He took no risks and was never seen in doubtful company in any public place.

He belonged to a few clubs, and they were not the kind of joint where a doll took it all off in a spot light or where a comic unloaded his blue patter. They were rather staid places, patronised by stockbrokers, lawyers, accountants and company directors, and sound market tips might be picked up over a brandy in the sedate bar.

Albert Raikes had accumulated his capital by questionable means, but some of his investments were real enough and legitimate enough to stop the Inland Revenue poking into his affairs too closely. Membership of the clubs helped his pose as an idle capitalist. His hands were clean and he kept his ear very close to the ground.

It was late in the afternoon when Nickie Preston came through on the phone and caught Albert Raikes in his flat. Nickie was reliable, usually. He passed on the information that a Sam Harris was trying to locate Ossie Trent and making a big business of it.

'Sam Harris?' said Raikes. 'I don't think I know him.'

'You wouldn't,' said Nickie. 'He's not in

your class. He's a twister, strictly small stuff, but he does get an idea once in a while.'

'Ossie Trent,' said Bertie thoughtfully. 'Did this Harris mug say what he wanted Ossie for?'

'He went all coy on me,' said Nickie. 'I said I'd put the word around. He'll be ringing me later. Maybe he's got something he thinks Ossie might handle. From what I know of Harris I wouldn't think that's very likely.'

'Life is full of surprises,' said Bertie. 'He might have got lucky, although we haven't heard of anybody doing anything recently. It might be as well to check on him, Nick. If he thinks it's worth Ossie Trent's while I'd like to know what it is.'

'This Harris,' said Nickie, 'it doesn't have a very good name if he's in it, Bertie. I never heard of a job that didn't blow up when he had part of it, you ask anybody – he is definitely bad news.'

'I am not proposing to take him into partnership,' said Raikes pleasantly. 'You rang me, Nick, and we both think the same thing. If there is any kind of a possible connection between Ossie Trent and this layabout we should know what it is. It could be interesting. Nobody looks for Trent unless they have some merchandise in mind.'

'Exactly my own thoughts,' said Nickie.
'Harris is nobody, but he's no fool.'

'When he rings fix a meeting,' said Raikes.
'It'll have to be private or we won't get anything out of him. Can we use your place? I wouldn't want him here.'

'No trouble,' said Nickie. 'It'll be private enough. I had this bird I was expecting over, but I can put her off.'

'I will be suitably grateful,' said Albert Raikes.

'Suppose Harris doesn't want to come?' said Nickie. 'He sounded kind of nervous on the phone.'

'Nickie,' said Raikes, 'if you can't talk this nonentity into doing what we want, you are not the man I have always taken you to be. I buy information, not excuses. Anybody who thinks he has urgent business with Ossie Trent interests me, so arrange to have this man at your place by seven this evening, and expect me there in time to set the scene before he arrives. Am I asking too much?'

'There may be nothing to it after all,' said Nickie.

'Then I won't be blaming you, and I have nothing of importance on hand for this evening. It will help to pass the time. Is Harris likely to turn violent?'

'Not a chance,' said Nickie, well aware of Bertie's dislike for any rough stuff while he was around. 'He's a mouse. I can coax something out of him if I get him here in my pad.'

'Tell him Trent is visiting you this evening,' said Raikes. 'That will bring him in a hurry.'

'Leave it with me,' said Nickie Preston. 'If there's any alteration I'll let you know right away.'

'Do that,' said Albert Raikes, and rang off.

8

In default of any other offers, Sam told Nickie Preston that he would be most happy to present himself at the Preston pad that evening around seven. In the back of his mind he thought it a little unlikely that Nickie Preston was going to produce Ossie Trent, just like that; but it was the only lead he had come across so far.

Nickie had some sort of a part-time job with a chain of betting offices, and he certainly seemed to move around a lot, and with money in his pocket. He just might have a line on the elusive Ossie, and there hadn't been a sniff anywhere else.

So Sam then rang Carrie to show her how diligent he was being on her business.

'I'm not promising anything,' he said. 'I know Nickie Preston and he doesn't owe me any favours.'

'I'll come with you,' she said.

'Not necessary,' he said. 'Nickie says he can put me in touch tonight with Ossie Trent, frankly I reckon he's having me on, but I'll find out, he's the kind of feller you have to watch pretty closely, I'll do it better on my own.'

'Sammie,' she said, and her voice was suddenly warm and friendly, 'I think I ought to be there, you don't have to protect me, and it's my headache, after all. Where do I pick you up?'

'You're a crazy girl,' he said. 'You think I'll fall down on the job.'

'You've done very well so far,' she said. 'I'd have been lost without you. Now just give me the time and the place.'

They met at the top end of Queensway, just a few minutes before seven. She was driving the blue Fiat, and she looked pretty good and happy, in dark blue trousers and a blue and white striped jersey with short sleeves.

'Clever Sammie,' she said as he slid in beside her. 'A man of many parts. I never expected such a quick result.'

'Don't kid yourself,' he said, 'it could be a dud.'

'Then we'll have to see, won't we?'

'You might need some cash,' he said. 'Nickie Preston likes to take a small percentage, he does nothing for nothing.'

She indicated her bag on the back seat. 'I come prepared. Where now, Sammie?'

They found an empty slot in a turning at the lower end of Queensway, in a row of Edwardian houses that had been looked after and preserved from decay, and chopped into spacious flats; there were iron balconies on some of the first floor windows and window boxes with flowers; it was still a good address, and handy to the West End proper.

Sam found Nickie Preston's number in the middle of the row, and rang his bell; there were six names against the bell pushes, and Nickie's was on the first floor.

He was waiting for them on the landing. He wore a black blazer with gilt buttons, skin-tight beige slacks and a striped cravat. He was not yet thirty, tall and a little too slender for his height; a lounging sort of young man, terribly pleased with his own appearance; he was, he considered, an excellent specimen of elegant masculinity.

He smiled as they came up the stairs. 'Nice of you to be so punctual, Sam,' he said. 'I rather thought you'd be alone…'

'This is Miss Carrie Thorpe,' said Sam. It had been Carrie's idea to use her maiden name, since she said it was better if Nickie Preston didn't connect their search for Ossie Trent with her husband – and she had failed to explain why to Sam. There hadn't been time to argue it out.

'Miss Thorpe shares an interest with me, sort of,' said Sam.

'Delightful,' Nickie murmured, his gaze automatically taking in Carrie's items of charm. 'Do come on in.'

He took them into a fair sized room over-looking the street. The furniture was good, and the room hadn't been hacked about with partitions to spoil its proportions.

Carrie gazed about her with approval. 'I like it,' she said.

'I'm so glad,' said Nickie. 'I'm really rather fond of it myself. Now what are we going to drink? An aperitif, Miss Thorpe? I happen to have a drinkable sherry.'

'Thank you,' said Carrie.

'You will prefer beer, if I recall correctly, Sam,' said Nickie Preston. 'Make yourselves comfortable and then we can proceed to our business.'

Sam grunted, not going too much on the social stuff, not with Nickie Preston – it was all bogus. He noted there were two doors leading into the room, one they had come in by, and another at the end, and it was slightly open – the bedroom or the bathroom? Or the kitchen?

Nickie was busy fixing the drinks at the cabinet, and Sam also noticed how he glanced a couple of times across at that partly open door, which had Sam wondering if there was anybody in there listening. He thought first of all that it might be a bird Nickie had tucked out of the way, because Nickie wasn't the kind of feller to be on his own in a plushy pad like this.

Sam's second thought was even more interesting: it might be Ossie Trent after all. Waiting to overhear just why Carrie was after him.

When Nickie brought over the drinks, Sam said, 'Okay if I use your bathroom, Nickie?' He had got up and was heading to that open door.

'This way,' said Nickie quickly, and opened the door they had come in by. 'Right opposite,' he said.

'Pardon me,' said Sam and padded across to the bathroom.

There was plenty of evidence in there that Nickie Preston entertained female guests. Nickie had left the sitting-room door open so Sam had to return the way he had left without any chance to nose about. And he rejoined the party just in time to hear Carrie say, 'but I thought you told Sammie he could see Ossie Trent here–'

–'Not quite as simple as that,' said Nickie.

'Why not?' said Carrie bluntly.

'Well now,' said Nickie, 'suppose you tell me just what your business is with Ossie, he is a very much sought after man.'

'So we gather,' said Carrie, and then added politely, 'my business is with him.'

'What's this then, Nickie?' said Sam. 'Ossie Trent is a high-class fence, we all know that – but I never heard he kept you as a body-guard or manager or whatever the hell you think you are.'

'I could be acting for him,' said Nickie. 'You have something to sell? It might be possible for me to introduce you, but I really must know what you have that you think might interest him.'

Carrie shook her head and smiled. 'I think you are wasting our time. I don't think you know anything about Oswald Trent.'

'I know where he is,' said Nickie, 'and you are much too charming to be calling me a liar.'

'Sweet of you to put it like that,' said Carrie, 'but my business with Trent is still personal, strictly personal.' Her handbag was in her lap. 'I am ready to pay for information, of course.'

'I just might find that a shade insulting,' said Nickie Preston.

'Now I reckon I've heard everything,' said Sam.

'What have you got and where did you get it?' said Nickie.

'Don't be silly,' said Carrie. 'How much do you want?'

'I could take your money and give you false information, have you thought of that?' said Nickie. 'So what are you hoping to sell to Ossie? You'll have to tell me in the end, or we'll be sitting here all night.'

'I think not,' said Carrie. She opened her bag, and it wasn't money she took out. It was a little automatic, very neat and compact, and she held it with the casual ease of one who had used it before. No dramatic waving about.

'I never knew you had one of those,' said Sam softly.

Carrie was still smiling across at Nickie Preston who was not making any kind of a move at all.

'Now look,' he said, 'we don't need any of that—'

'I could put one slap in your middle,' said Carrie. 'I'd say you tried to assault me and Sam here would back me up. Right, Sam?'

'You can bet on it,' said Sam, and he was observing her little gun with considerable care. 'If he lifts a finger against you I'll scream bloody murder – you sure you can handle that thing?'

'Very sure,' said Carrie calmly. 'It just makes a little hole, and not a lot of noise.'

'Handy,' said Sam.

'And lethal,' said Carrie. 'If we turned the radio on nobody would hear a thing.'

'This is ridiculous,' said Nickie Preston, his voice rising. 'You can't frighten me with that thing, put it away and I'll tell you where you'll find Trent.'

'I have a better idea,' said Carrie. 'You'll come with us and show us, and then there won't be any silly mistakes.'

'No!' Nickie began to make a hesitant move towards Carrie.

She was on her feet in an instant, a tight little smile on her face. She slammed the gun into Nickie's middle and shoved him back until he stood against the wall, and she had been so quick and decisive that he had made no attempt to wrestle with her for the gun that cut so wickedly into his stomach.

'God,' he whispered, his hands flopping uselessly and his head rolling back against the wall. 'Don't do that – for God's sake, don't do it...'

'Carrie, baby,' said Sam nervously, keeping clear of the scene of conflict. 'You got him scared ... take it easy, baby.'

Nickie Preston had his eyes screwed up. She really was leaning in on that gun, and when he sucked in his breath he almost felt the metal touch his backbone. And he didn't have the nerve to move a hand and touch her. Her face was so close that he felt her warm breath on his cheek, and in other circumstances the scent of her body and her nearness would have been provocative. Now it just added to his panic.

'I think we're getting somewhere,' said Carrie.

'Looks like it,' said Sam. He was still nervous about that gun. 'Watch it, Carrie – he's ready to fold...'

Carrie gave the gun an extra shove, which drew a deep grunt from Nickie who had been trying so hard to tuck his belly in so as to lessen the target area.

With her free hand Carrie tapped his sweaty cheek, using just the tips of her fingers fastidiously.

'Are you listening to me, Nickie?'

Nickie nodded, his eyes still closed and his hands flopping uselessly at his side. 'God ... you're hurting me...'

'I hope so,' said Carrie.

The door that had been partly open now swung back wide, and for a moment Albert Raikes stood there. Then with a sudden spurt he made for the other door across the room. In his neat grey suiting he looked like a startled cleric in civvies caught in a knocking-shop. He was not built for rapid movement and ran clumsily into a chair and almost fell flat on his face.

'Get him, Sam!' Carrie snapped. 'Stop him!'

Sam guessed this couldn't be Ossie Trent because Ossie was tall and slim and this feller was fat and much too old, and the fact that he was running away encouraged Sam to take the offensive in a manner that was not usual for him.

With a singularly ungraceful leap he landed on the fugitive's back and wrapped his arms around him with such force that Albert's face came into sharp contact with the frame of the door. Sam moved clear and Albert slid to the floor and began to moan into the carpet.

Sam turned him over. Albert was bleeding from his nose and his mouth, and he was trying painfully to spit out the shattered teeth from his upper plate. The shock to his system had been devastating. Not in all his life before had he been roughed up like this.

'I don't reckon he'll do much more running,' said Sam. 'I don't know him but he isn't Ossie Trent.'

'Bring him over here,' said Carrie.

Nickie hadn't budged for the very good reason that Carrie still had him pinned against the wall. She was clearly a girl with wonderful powers of concentration.

Sam gave Albert a toe in the ribs and yanked him across the carpet. Albert was too shaken to offer any kind of resistance. He rolled over on his side and took out a nice white handkerchief and put it to his mouth very tenderly.

'Who is he?' Carrie demanded.

Nickie Preston swallowed. For a fleeting moment when Raikes appeared there had been a slender hope of getting out of this crazy situation. If that bloody woman had only turned away for a second with that gun–

'He's a friend of mine,' said Nickie.

'So he hides behind the door,' said Sam. 'It's a set-up. What's the gag, Nickie?'

Nickie said nothing. Carrie inspected the casualty. He was in a very distressed condition.

'What's his name?' she said.

'Albert Raikes.'

Carrie glanced at Sam. He shook his head. 'Never heard of him. Why didn't you produce him when we came up here, Nickie?'

'It was his idea,' said Nickie.

'There's a bad smell around here,' said Sam. 'Why did he try to run for it?'

'He doesn't like guns,' said Nickie. 'Neither do I. Sammie, ask the lady to take it easy will you?'

'She doesn't take orders from me,' said Sam. 'You never heard of women's lib? Is this feller your boss?'

'No,' said Nickie.

'Just a mate who happened to be here when we arrived so he hides behind the door and hears all we say,' said Sam. 'Then he gets shy on account of there's a lady with a gun. You can get yourself knotted, Nickie Preston. We don't buy that load of cobblers, boyo.'

'Sammie,' said Carrie. She had stepped back but she kept her little gun lined up on Nicke's middle. 'Can you fix up that one on the floor? We can't have him at liberty when we leave.'

'My pleasure,' said Sam.

'Stick him in the bathroom,' said Carrie.

'Right away, baby,' said Sam. This was another new aspect of Carrie. No argument. Do it chop-chop.

Albert Raikes began to protest but very feebly when Sam dragged him across the floor to the door. Sam kicked the door open masterfully, heaved Raikes out into the hall and across into the bathroom.

Raikes tried to stand but his legs wouldn't do it, and he slumped onto the lavatory pedestal and made unhappy noises, his eyes pleading with Sam.

'You heard the lady,' said Sam.

Albert Raikes mumbled something, and the movement of his lips made him wince. He slid a trembling hand inside his jacket and Sam got ready to clobber him again.

Raikes held out his wallet, opened it clumsily, took out the notes and offered them to Sam.

'Bribery,' said Sam. 'That's real bad. I ought to be insulted.'

He took the money and stuffed it into his pocket. 'You haven't bought yourself anything, dad.' He gave Raikes a reproachful smile.

He made him kneel by the bath and used a couple of towels knotted together to tie his legs. The medicine cupboard yielded a bandage and a packet of elastoplasts. With the bandage he tied Raikes's hands behind his back. He tipped him over on his side, and taped a damp flannel across his mouth with strips of elastoplast.

Raikes could breathe and he wouldn't choke on his own saliva, but any shouting he tried to do would bring him nothing but more grief.

'When we've finished with Nickie we'll send him back,' said Sam. 'So you'd better hope we don't have to keep him too long.'

Albert Raikes was beyond coherent speech. Sam took the key and locked the door from the outside just in case Raikes worked a miracle and got free. Then Sam slipped the key in his pocket. Very tidy so far.

9

In the interval Carrie had allowed Nickie to sit, but she had placed herself between him and the door, and it was clear that Nickie wasn't intending to try anything heroic or adventurous. With one hand he was massaging his middle where the gun had dug in, and on his normally handsome face there was an expression of extreme caution mingled with much uneasiness.

Being held up by a woman with a gun in his own sitting-room was an unforgettable experience, and he had seen what had happened to Albert.

'You must be needing Ossie Trent pretty badly to put on a show like this,' he said.

'You'd better go on believing just that,' said Carrie.

'We could arrange this in a friendly fashion,' he said.

'I don't know any reason why we should,' she said. 'You had that fat snooper hiding behind the door, that doesn't suggest to me that I can trust you, so we will continue to do it my way.'

'Suppose I got up and walked over to that door?' said Nickie.

'Okay,' said Carrie, 'if you think you can make it, try it.'

'You're bluffing,' he said. 'You wouldn't shoot.'

'You'll never get a better chance to find out,' she said.

'You wouldn't do it,' he said, but he didn't move from his chair.

Carrie pursed her lips and swung the little gun up so that it pointed at his chest. 'If I'm bluffing why don't you call me on it?'

He exhaled noisily. 'You're a bitch.'

'And a very good shot as well,' she said. 'Do I get some action?'

A woman with a gun in her hand was highly unpredictable at the best of times, and Nickie was sure this one knew what she was doing. She was sharp and in control and she wasn't bluffing.

Sam came back. 'One fat gent safely stowed,' he said.

'He has a heart condition,' said Nickie. 'If he snuffs it in there–'

–'On your feet,' said Carrie.

Nickie Preston stood up slowly.

'Now I'll explain how we're gong to leave,'

said Carrie. 'Sam, you'll go first, and when we get down to the car you'll do the driving. Nickie here will be the meat in the sandwich. I will be half a step behind him with my little shooter trained on the middle of his back in case he does anything I don't like, and I'll be so close that I couldn't possibly miss. Do we all understand the position?'

'A doddle,' said Sam.

Nickie Preston said nothing.

'We want very little from you but we want it now,' said Carrie. 'Sensible co-operation, and then we will part the best of friends.'

'I doubt that,' said Nickie. He glanced at the gun. 'Do you always threaten your friends with a gun?'

'I'm just being careful,' she said pleasantly. 'You said you knew where to find Ossie Trent. I think you're a liar, but we're going to find out. If I'm wrong I'll apologise. We'll move out now, Sammie.'

The door bell chimed. Of the three of them Carrie seemed the least perturbed. Sam swore softly. Carrie lifted one hand for silence. Nobody moved.

'Wait,' said Carrie softly.

The bell chimed its *ding-dong,* twice over.

'Nickie,' said Carrie, 'are you expecting anybody?'

Nickie was far from happy at this interruption because once again Carrie had closed up on him and that damned gun was sticking into his belly.

'I can't think of anybody,' he said.

'I bet it's a bird,' said Sam.

The bell chimed on and on. Nickie waited for Carrie to tell him what to do. And they all listened.

'Nickie,' said Carrie calmly, 'you'll have to get rid of whoever it is. Use your head and don't try to be clever because I'll be standing behind the door beside you.'

She took him out into the hall, then she placed herself by the wall so that she wouldn't be seen when the door was opened. She waved to Sam to get out of sight. The gun was in the pocket of her slacks and her hand was on it. She nodded at Nickie and he opened the door.

'My God, Nickie,' said a shrill female voice, 'you took your time about that! Did I get you out of bed?'

'I'm sorry, Lindy,' said Nickie. 'I didn't hear the bell.' He stood right in the doorway, holding the door.

Lindy was a smallish girl with a compact body and sturdy legs. She looked full of energy and indignation. She wore a red and white pinafore type dress that helped her to appear little more than a girlish seventeen, whereas she was in fact twenty-eight and had a divorce behind her. She could dance a little and make singing noises, and scratched a living of sorts on the fringes of show business.

'Didn't hear it?' she said. 'You gone deaf, Nickie?'

She pressed the bell again to prove her point.

'Sorry,' he said and sounded very awkward.

She leaned a chunky hip against the frame of the door. 'When you phoned and said you couldn't see me this evening,' she said, 'I wondered just what business it was that had come up so urgently.'

'As a matter of fact I'm on the way out now,' he said.

'You're nervous,' she said conversationally. 'I wonder why? It couldn't be because of little me, could it? Are you cooking up something I shouldn't know about?'

'Now you're being silly,' he said. 'Listen, Lindy, I really am in a most frightful hurry–'

'In too much of a hurry to invite me in for a little drink?'

He was shifting around on his feet, the picture of indecision.

'I'm sorry,' he repeated. 'It's terribly inconvenient, Lindy – and I do have to rush–'

'I'll remember that,' she said, 'the next time you think you might like me in bed for a quick lay.'

'Please,' he said, 'I'm really pushed for time this evening, Lindy darling–'

–'Don't darling me,' she said. 'If only you could see what a drip you look standing there saying how terribly sorry I can't come into your lousy flat!'

Nickie tried to smile. Lindy was celebrated for her uninhibited outbursts. She could whip herself into a fury at the slightest provocation when the mood was on her.

'Do listen, Lindy,' he said in some desperation, 'I'll ring you tomorrow and we'll have dinner–'

'That's big of you,' she said acidly.

'Tomorrow,' he said quickly. 'That's a firm date, I'll call round for you, okay?'

She hadn't moved, and he made the elementary mistake of trying to close the door on her, so she stuck her foot in the way. And to hell with feminine dignity.

'You've got somebody in there with you,' she called through the opening. 'I know bloody well you have. What's she got that's so special, Nickie? Three boobs and a wall-eye?'

Carrie moved away from her cover by the wall. She tapped Nickie on the shoulder and presented herself in the open doorway.

'I have just the normal equipment, my dear,' she said. 'And there's nothing wrong with my sight.'

Lindy inspected her, experiencing the futile envy of a stocky girl for one whose lissom contours would be for ever beyond her no matter how rigorously she dieted.

For a moment the atmosphere was electric, and Nickie waited for Lindy to dredge up some of her coarsest comments.

'So you're the urgent business,' she said.

'Just good friends,' said Carrie. 'I'm not trespassing.'

Lindy transferred her attention to Nickie and her eyes were bright with hostility.

'Don't blame Nickie,' said Carrie pleasantly. 'We had some urgent business to discuss. It's all my fault and I'm sorry if I've interrupted anything.'

'He's a lying bastard and you're welcome to him,' said Lindy. She swung round and stumped vigorously down the stairs, and they heard her slam the front door.

From the bathroom came some muffled bumping noises which would surely have aroused Lindy's curiosity if she had heard them while she was at the door.

'We'll give her a couple of minutes,' said Carrie. 'Is she likely to hang around outside?'

'I don't think so,' said Nickie. 'But you never can tell with Lindy.'

Sam emerged from the sitting-room. 'That's one bird you can now cross off your list, Nickie,' he said cheerfully. 'She won't be doing you any favours any more.'

'You are a vulgar little shyster,' said Nickie.

The bathroom door bumped and rattled. And they all looked at it.

'Get him quiet in there,' said Carrie, 'then we can be on our way. And you, Nickie, you can shut up from now on until I tell you to speak.'

'I hope I meet you one day when you don't have that gun,' said Nickie. 'It would give me much pleasure to rearrange your face.'

'That's fighting talk, boyo,' said Sam.

'Never mind him, Sam,' said Carrie. 'See to that old fool in there.'

Sam went over, unlocked the bathroom door and pushed at it. It moved back a foot or so and then stuck.

'He's got himself wedged up against it,' said Sam. 'Come and give me a hand, Nickie.'

'Why the hell should I?' said Nickie. 'It's

your idea, not mine.'

They were brave words, but he incautiously looked at Sam as he spoke. Carrie's intervention was quick and precise. With that little gun clubbed in her fist she hit Nickie smartly behind his left ear. Just once was enough. He staggered and grunted.

'Now move,' said Carrie.

Nickie moved, whispering to himself and holding his head.

'Daft as a brush,' said Sam. 'Now let's have a shove.'

Between them they eased the door back far enough for them to step inside and over the body of Albert Raikes. He was making gurgling sounds through that flannel over his mouth and his colour was high.

'You'll strain yourself, dad,' said Sam. 'With a bad heart you shouldn't go in for acrobatics, so why don't you relax like a sensible old feller? Nickie, you grab his feet and we'll dump him in the bath, that'll hold him still. If he creates any more I'll turn the cold tap on – you hear that, old man?'

Albert's eyes bulged and his head wagged from side to side. They straightened him out on the floor and lifted him into the bath.

'Sammie,' Nickie whispered, 'listen, let's make a deal, we can take that bitch out there and Raikes will see us right afterwards … what do you say? We can jump her between us…'

'You don't learn very fast,' said Sam. 'I'm on the opposition and I'm staying there. You made a daft move when you had this feller hiding behind the door, I don't call that very friendly–'

–'But I can explain that–'

'Get stuffed,' said Sam. 'I'm not interested.'

'Thank you, Sammie,' said Carrie from the doorway. 'I heard all that. He really is a nasty piece of work.'

'She's making a mug out of you, Sam,' said Nickie.

'If you don't watch out you'll get another crack on the noggin,' said Sam.

They left Albert Raikes in a semi-sitting position in the bath, facing the taps. He looked a very sad and impotent little man.

Sam locked the door. 'Remind me to give you the key before we part company, Nickie,' he said. 'We wouldn't want the old buzzard to get himself into a real mess, now would we?'

They left in formation, as Carrie had instructed, and on the way down the short

144

flight of stairs they met nobody so there was no need to pretend that they were all friends together.

Out on the pavement Carrie gave Sam the keys of the car, and at no time did her watchful gaze leave Nickie's sullen face. He didn't think she would use that gun out there on the public street, but he wasn't prepared to risk finding out. His head ached, and all the time Carrie was standing so close to him in a position that was very nearly indecent.

There was no sign of Lindy. Just the parked cars. And a middle-aged woman who was out walking her dog and took no notice of them. A placid summer evening.

'In,' said Carrie. She got in beside him in the back, she took the gun out of her pocket and held it in her lap, turning sideways so as to face him.

'Ossie Trent,' she said. 'You know where I can find him, so take me there.'

He gave her a speculative look. 'Who's backing you? You're not working on your own, and you're too smart to be depending on a no-hoper like Sam Harris.'

'Are you offering to join me?' said Carrie sweetly.

'You could do worse,' said Nickie.

Sam had started the engine, now he

switched it off and listened with both ears flapping.

'You hear that, Sammie?' said Carrie.

'Bloody nerve,' said Sam.

'If he's the best you can do,' said Nickie, 'I don't fancy Ossie Trent will be all that happy to see you. He doesn't handle trash.'

'You're being very liberal with your insults this evening,' said Carrie.

'I've never heard of you,' said Nickie. 'I know all the people who matter, the kind of people Ossie Trent does business with. You don't fit.'

'Drive, Sammie, just start,' said Carrie. As the car pulled away she reversed the gun with the deftness of a juggler and rapped Nickie sharply on the thigh, above his knee-cap, and sat well away from him as he stiffened with pain and cupped both hands over his numbed leg.

'You are a bitch!' he whispered.

'I warned you, boyo,' said Sam. He was driving with his usual flashy skill. In default of any other directions he was heading back up to the Bayswater Road.

There was a silence from the back seat. Nickie was brooding over his bruised thigh, and he didn't want to look at Carrie any more, but he knew she was smiling at him.

The streets were crowded and there was safety all around him, but not inside that damned little car with her beside him. He was wishing he had never let Raikes push him into this. That woman with her vicious habits was an unknown quantity. And he was getting no comfort from the back view of Sam Harris because nobody with any sense would ever trust that no-good chiseller.

'Right,' said Carrie. 'Now for some co-operation.'

'And what do I get out of it?' said Nickie.

'Liberty,' said Carrie, smiling. 'Isn't that enough?'

'You're crazy,' he said. 'This is London, you can't seriously hope to get away with a kidnapping job.'

'You don't read the papers,' said Carrie.

'It's not on,' said Nickie. 'You're fooling with me.'

'If I gave Sammie the word,' she said, 'we'd drive out into the country somewhere quiet, and I have just the place in mind. The way Sammie drives it wouldn't take us long. Just the three of us. You can fill in the rest of it for yourself.'

Nickie made himself look at her, and she was smiling.

'Sammie will take us by the back roads so

we won't have to wait for any traffic lights, in case you get any heroic ideas about jumping.'

She slid up close against him, linked her left arm in his right, and in her right hand the gun pressed against his side, hidden from outside view by the entwined arms.

'I will hate it if I have to hurt you again,' she said. 'It offends my womanly tenderness.'

Sam laughed from the front seat.

'Trent isn't easy to find,' said Nickie. 'He uses a number of addresses.'

'Where do we start?' said Carrie.

10

Their first call was across the Park, to a large and unlovely block of flatlets near the Albert Hall. Accommodation units in a good address, suitable at the most for two people and no kids or pets. A location where you wouldn't have to know your neighbours if you didn't want to.

There were three entrances, with the names of the tenants slotted in on a board, one for each slice of the building.

There was a porter's office in the middle

entrance, but he was not around when they arrived, so they foraged without him. Oswald Trent's name appeared on the last list they checked. He was on the very top floor.

The three of them filled the lift. They stood waiting outside Trent's door and Carrie rang the bell at the very end of a quiet corridor. There was no answer, and they waited long after it was clear there was going to be no answer. And Ossie Trent's name did not appear in the telephone directory.

'I told you he wasn't easy to find,' said Nickie. 'We could spend all night at it and get nothing.'

'We've got all night, and more,' Carrie told him. She took him back down to the car and Sam went in search of the porter.

He found him in a semi-basement room beside the underground parking area. He was having his supper, a pork pie and a bottle of stout. A small colour television set was working in a corner.

Sam explained what he wanted. The porter turned down the sound of the television set but left the picture. It needed adjusting.

'Mr Trent? Haven't seen him for a couple of weeks. We got over two hundred tenants in the building, I can't be expected to keep tabs on all of them, now can I? What you want him for, mate?'

'Just business,' said Sam.

'That's a funny thing,' said the porter, 'there was this American feller here yesterday, he was looking for Mr Trent and he said the same as you – business. And I told him the same as I'm telling you.'

'You've no idea where I might contact Ossie Trent?' said Sam.

'I been through all this before yesterday with that Yank,' said the porter. 'I don't get paid to watch all the tenants coming in and out.'

Sam agreed that was a reasonable attitude. The porter turned up the sound on his set to indicate the conference was over. Sam left and went back to the car.

'He hasn't been there for a couple of weeks. There's a Yank looking for him as well.'

'He worked over there,' said Nickie. 'Made a packet of money, so I hear.'

'Now the next one, Nickie,' said Carrie. 'Ossie Trent may be elusive, but he has to settle somewhere.'

'There's a private hotel in the Gloucester Road,' said Nickie. 'He stays there sometimes.'

They drew a complete blank there as well.

Carrie had done the asking, while Sam kept Nickie company in the car, and Nickie was by now too dispirited to offer Sam any argument; Carrie had left her gun with Sam.

Carrie had an unfruitful conversation with the hotel manageress, a formidable lady of much refinement. She was emphatic that no gentleman named Oswald Trent had ever been a resident at the hotel and she had been managing it for some eight years. Her manner made it clear she didn't think Carrie might be any better than she should be, asking after a guest who didn't exist.

The respectable evening traffic swirled along the Gloucester Road. And Sam complained that he was getting hungry.

'If Ossie Trent has been using a false name too often we don't have a hope in hell of finding him,' he said. 'Are you having us on a string, Nickie?'

'I'm doing the best I can,' said Nickie sourly. 'You don't imagine I'm enjoying this, do you?'

'Do some more thinking, Nickie,' said Carrie. 'There has to be a place where Ossie Trent hangs his hat. What about his women? There's a woman somewhere, isn't there? Think, Nickie.'

'What the hell do you think I'm doing?' he said savagely. 'And it's no use prodding me with that gun, that doesn't help. There's somebody I could try, but it'll have to be on the phone.'

Sam drove them to a kiosk. Carrie went with Nickie and stood by him with the door propped open. What could look nicer than two young folk sharing a phone call in such a friendly fashion?

'I don't want to do this,' said Nickie, quite unhappily. 'It could get me into serious trouble.'

'You're in that now,' said Carrie, 'or hadn't you noticed? Who are you calling?'

Nickie didn't reply. He began to dial.

'Hold the receiver out so that I can hear,' said Carrie.

They heard the phone ringing. Nickie's face was damp and he was moistening his lips.

A man's voice said, 'Yes?'

Nickie put his money in. In little more than a whisper, he said, 'Harry, this is Nickie Preston – don't ring off – I have to find Ossie Trent in a hurry–'

–'Pretty boy Preston, asking me a favour! This really is a surprise–'

'Harry, it's urgent–'

152

'Sonnie, I wouldn't cross the street to save your life. The next time I see you I'll mark you so's your own mother won't know you. You have my solemn word on that. Now don't bother me unless you can come up with the cash.'

The line went dead.

'Well that didn't get us very far,' said Carrie. 'I gather Harry doesn't like you awfully much because you owe him some money, correct?'

'It was a little deal that blew up,' said Nickie sullenly. 'He thinks I took him for a ride. It was just a bit of bad luck. He does a lot of business with Ossie Trent. He'll know where to contact him, but you heard what he said, I'm not going to have anything more to do with it and I don't give a damn about the gun in your pocket. He's a vicious character and I'm not going anywhere near him.'

'Now you really are scared,' said Carrie. 'You should have mentioned him earlier, is he the Big Brain?'

'Big enough,' said Nickie. 'That was Harry Fergus.'

'Call him again,' she said. 'I'll talk to him.'

She took the receiver from Nickie and shoved him against the glass panel.

Nickie found a coin. 'It won't do you any good,' he said.

'Don't bet on it,' said Carrie.

When the connection had been made she said, 'Nickie Preston has just spoken to you, Mr Fergus. I'm with him–'

–'Madam, I cannot congratulate you on the company you keep. Watch your handbag while he's around, and anything else you may have of value–'

–'I am Carrie Newland,' she said.

There was a pause.

'Tommy Newland is my husband,' she said. 'You probably know him.'

'I do. Indeed I do. I begin to appreciate your position, Mrs Newland. But you should still choose your associates more wisely. Tommy might be distressed to hear you are with a young louse like Preston, if you will excuse the expression.'

'You are so right, Mr Fergus, but there's nothing like that about it.' She smiled at Nickie who could hear none of the conversation because she had the receiver tight against her ear.

'I am relieved to hear it,' said Harry Fergus. 'I have some regard for your husband, he had the bad luck he did not deserve.'

'Ossie Trent,' she said. 'I've been trying to

get in touch with him, can you help me, please?'

There was another short silence.

'I think you should come and see me, Mrs Newland. Preston will give you the directions, but don't bring him with you because I would not like to have to deal with him in front of a lady.'

'Thank you,' she said.

'I will be waiting for you,' he said.

Carrie put the receiver down. 'Harry Fergus is waiting for me to visit him,' she said. 'You are to give me directions but I'm not to bring you unless I want to see you roughly handled, and I don't think I want that.'

'Nice of you,' said Nickie. 'You should have told me Tommy Newland was your husband, I might have been more ready to co-operate.'

'The address,' she said firmly.

'He lives in Weybridge, the house stands on its own near the bridge, with the gardens going down to the Wey. It's called Rosemount. Anybody down there will show you where it is.'

They had moved out of the kiosk. Nickie wiped his face with the heel of his hand.

'I hope I never see you again,' he said.

'Harry Fergus called you a louse,' she said

pleasantly. 'He must know you very well. Now run along and liberate that old boy in your bath.'

Nickie Preston straightened himself and thought how easy it was to dislike intensely an attractive woman when she had spent the evening chasing you around the town and sticking you in the belly with a gun.

'You're too tricky,' he said. 'If I'd known you were Tommy Newland's wife you wouldn't have needed that silly little gun.'

Carrie smiled very prettily. 'For your information, Nickie, it isn't loaded – just window-dressing. Effective, wasn't it?'

He glared after her, but it was too late to tell her just what he thought because she was moving briskly across the pavement to the car.

She slipped in beside Sam. 'Have you ever heard of Harry Fergus? We are about to call on him.'

'We're moving up a notch,' said Sam. 'Harry Fergus operates in a big way. I've never seen the feller on account of he's right out of my class, but I know he runs a big organisation with plenty of brains and cash behind it.'

'Weybridge, Sammie,' she said, 'as smartly as you can.'

11

As a result of a phone call late that afternoon, Ossie Trent had met an associate in the lounge of a quiet and sedate hotel in the West End. It was one of their favoured meeting places, because nobody in their line of business would be expected to use the place, and thus there was little danger of any of the fuzz drifting in to wonder what they were cooking up.

Harry Fergus was a solid figure of a middle-aged citizen, evidently prosperous and respectable. His hair was silvery grey, he had a snug little paunch, his manner was mild and outwardly benign, and he had a warming smile that invited confidence.

The real Harry Fergus was something quite different. In recent years he had been in effective control of an organisation that had given the Fraud Squad and the experts of the Serious Crimes Squad some very serious headaches. He had brains and resources; he thought big, and took no chances.

He and Ossie had done business together,

157

and they had a respect for each other's talent. Now that old Rufus Whittaker had shuffled off this mortal coil, Ossie felt that Harry was about the only man he knew in London worth trusting.

They took tea together, a pair of obviously respectable men of affairs; company directors, no doubt; probably senior partners in well-reputed firms; pillars of the Money Establishment.

'Ossie,' said Harry in his soft unemphatic voice, 'there's been a Yank in town asking for you. He's a hard boy and he's ready to spend money. Italian American type.'

'Does he give a name?' said Ossie. He was stirring his tea and his heart had skipped a beat.

'No name,' said Harry. 'I thought you ought to know. He's a hatchet-man if ever I saw one. Been here three days now, nosing around. You must have left some unfinished business over there, correct?'

Ossie shrugged, thinking hard and fast.

'He's serious and he wants you, Ossie,' said Harry. 'You want to meet him?'

Ossie smiled very faintly.

'That's what I thought,' said Harry. 'If you stay around here long enough he'll catch up with you. Some conniving bastard will give him the tip. You ought to go invisible for a while, Ossie. Let him get tired of looking.'

'I'll do that,' said Ossie. 'I am very much obliged to you, Harry.'

'It's nothing,' said Harry. 'We can't have you shot up by some bloody Yank. Bad for business. Would you like me to have a couple of my chaps look after this lad? I could quote you a cut-price, as between friends.'

It was a strange offer to be made in those genteel surroundings, and it would have appalled the good people at the neighbouring tables.

Ossie's smile became a little firmer. 'Not necessary, Harry, but thanks for the suggestion. I'll drive down to the cottage at Hungerford and wait it out there. You know the place and you've got the number, so we can keep in touch.'

'Go fishing and don't hurry back,' said Harry. It seemed like very sound advice, since in Ossie's mind there was little doubt about what this visitor was after. Harry's guess had been right. The 'unfinished business' could be connected with those stocks and bonds Joey had left with him, and now converted into cash for his own purposes.

There could have been some kind of a

record – Joey always knew what he was worth. So suppose this tough character had been sent across to collect, to square the account? It was not impossible. It had been in the back of his mind, something he hoped would never happen. It was not at all a healthy prospect.

He rang Laura and explained that he would be unable to see her for a few days. There was a bit of a tricky problem that he had to get sorted out, and he had to be on his own to concentrate. It was just one of those business tangles, it would bore her if he tried to explain, but it had blown up quite unexpectedly. He was apologetic and convincing.

'I'll be at the Hungerford cottage,' he said. 'It's the only place I know where I won't be interrupted ... think of me up to my ears in it – reports and balance sheets and bank statements and so forth – terribly boring and tiresome, but I can't get out of it.'

'Poor old you,' she said. 'I have some pleasant recollections of the cottage.'

'I'd ask you to come with me,' he said, 'but you'd be a disturbing influence, and I'd never get any work done.'

'I like the way you put that,' she said. 'Don't knock yourself out – somehow I can't see you as a harassed tycoon.'

'Not me,' said Ossie. 'Tycoons have hordes of underlings to do the sweating, I have to do my own. As soon as I see daylight I'll ring you.'

'Don't be too long,' she said. 'I've got into the habit of you.'

'Me too,' he said.

Rosemount was a spacious red-brick villa with a short drive in off a tree-lined avenue. An attractive property in a good neighbour-hood. Tidy and well maintained. There were plenty of flowers, mostly roses, of course.

Harry Fergus came out to meet them as soon as the car stopped. A gentleman at leisure in a beige cardigan in place of a jacket, with an unlit pipe in one hand.

'Mrs Newland,' he said, taking her by the arm, 'so very nice to see you.' He glanced at Sam who was a few paces in the rear.

'This is Sam Harris,' said Carrie. 'He's been helping me.'

Harry gave Sam a nod. He had met plenty like Sam Harris. The hangers-on. The blokes who ran the errands.

He took them in through a hall with some good pieces of furniture and into a room at the back of the house. There were french windows looking out over the gentle slope of a lawn, down to where the willows leaned over the river. It was dusk and very peaceful.

Sam was making his customary inventory of the room. There was plenty of stuff there that had cost a packet, but he didn't reckon Harry Fergus would have forked out much for it.

'First of all, to set your mind at rest, my dear,' said Harry, addressing himself to Carrie, 'we are alone here. My wife is playing bridge, and I have given the domestic staff the evening off, so we will not be disturbed. Now what will you drink?'

Carrie said whisky and Sam said it would suit him as well. Harry poured the drinks and pushed over a silver cigarette box so they could reach it on a low table between their chairs. He sat facing them. He smiled at Carrie, inviting her to begin.

'If you can tell me where I can get in touch with Ossie Trent I will be more than grateful,' she said.

'I was with him this afternoon,' said Harry. 'I happen to know he is not in London now. Your business with him must be urgent, Mrs Newland.'

'It is,' she said.

'You don't feel free to discuss it with me in

front of a third party?'

Sam cuddled his drink. This was where he should offer to retire. Carrie caught his eye and he grinned. He didn't think she would throw him out now, not after the events of the evening.

She didn't.

'I want to put some questions to Ossie Trent,' she said, 'about my husband, and what happened to the jewellery he had stolen a few hours before they arrested him.'

'And what does Tommy say?' said Harry in his soft friendly voice.

'Nothing,' she said. 'We are separated, he won't tell me anything. I've asked him. So I want to ask Ossie Trent. Tommy dealt with him. There was time before Tommy was arrested for him to pass the jewellery to Ossie Trent, or to drop it somewhere where Trent could pick it up later. I've a right at least to a share of what the stuff was worth.'

'A reasonable view,' said Harry.

'I need the money,' she said. 'The jewellery has never been found, Tommy won't talk to me when I visit him, we are not on good terms, unfortunately. I'm hoping Ossie Trent can give me some satisfaction, the jewellery was worth handling, Tommy didn't take rubbish.'

'Worth fifty thousand quid,' said Sam. 'There ought to be plenty left over even after a fence like Ossie Trent has taken his cut.'

Harry stroked the bowl of his pipe thoughtfully. 'Tommy has over four years to do, right?' he said.

Carrie nodded. 'I have to have some money, that's why I've been running all over the place trying to get hold of Ossie Trent – if he handled the jewellery I want to know where the money went.'

'He wouldn't cheat you,' said Harry.

'I hope not,' she said.

'He may know nothing about it.'

'I'd prefer to find that out for myself,' she said. 'I've got the chance to buy myself into a business, a legitimate business.'

Harry Fergus smiled. 'Ossie Trent is at a cottage in Hungerford, it's called Little End, it's on the edge of the common. He went there this evening. If he has any money that you ought to have I'm sure he'll pass it over.'

Carrie got to her feet. 'Thank you very much,' she said. 'Are you fit for the road, Sammie?'

Sam finished his drink and stood up. Harry ushered them out. And when they had gone he rang Ossie's Hungerford number and got no reply. Ossie would probably be having dinner at one of the town's hotels. He would not be exactly exhilarated when the forthright and energetic Mrs Newland arrived and demanded satisfaction. He would be jittery enough without that.

Harry thought it highly unlikely that Ossie had pulled a fast one over Tommy Newland. It wasn't his style. But then Tommy was in jail and that might have made a difference. There was a handy piece of cash involved. Harry decided he would leave it and let Ossie cope.

Less than an hour after Ossie had told her that he was going to be out of circulation for a while, Laura answered a ring at her front door.

A very polite young man in a sombre suit smiled at her and showed nice even white teeth. He had dark eyes and the stocky build that was reputed to be the mark of a sexual athlete – muscular and tireless. He held his hat in his hand, sort of over his heart, and he actually gave her a little bow.

'Please excuse me,' he said, 'but are you Miss Laura Heydon? The friend of Mr Oswald Trent?'

She smiled, it was all so deliciously formal. 'Yes,' she said. He couldn't possibly be selling anything.

'I am Don Vives,' he said. 'I am a stranger in London. I have urgent business that I must discuss with Mr Trent, I have spoken to many friends of his here, and they tell me you may know where I can find him. It is most important or I would not make this intrusion on you.'

There was more of that smile, and those dark eyes flicked over her in frank appraisal that told her how entrancing he found her.

'What a pity,' she said. 'You've just missed him. He's staying at his country cottage for a few days. Was he expecting you?'

'No,' said Don Vives. 'I just flew in from the States to arrange a business matter with Mr Trent. I would not like to go back without seeing him.'

'I can give you his address,' she said.

'You are being most kind,' he said, his eyes assessing the quality of her breasts.

If she invited him in she thought there was no knowing what might happen. And it wouldn't be rape. Yet he hadn't moved from that deferential stance in her doorway.

'He's at a place called Hungerford, that's in Berkshire,' she said. 'The cottage is by the common, it's called Little End, any of the locals will show you where it is. You could drive down there tomorrow morning and surprise him.'

'Ma'am, I might just do that.'

'Or I could ring him and let him know you're coming, that might be a better idea, don't you think? It's Mr Don Ives from America, is that right? Ossie was in the States for a while–'

She was being so helpful. Then he moved in on her, and as she backed away he kicked the door shut behind him.

'Now wait a minute,' she said–

He dropped his hat, his left arm went hard around her waist, and his right hand was on her throat. This could be no prelude to rape.

'You call nobody,' he said right into her face. He forced her neck back and back, and she couldn't use her arms because he had pinned them to her sides, and he was hard and strong. When she tried to kick him he thrust her against the wall and rammed his thighs tight into her so that she couldn't move.

He whispered something, but her ears were filled with the pounding of her blood. Her eyes rolled and her mouth gaped, and the unrelenting pressure of his hand on her throat was squeezing the life from her.

When she was limp and still he carried her into the bathroom. He ran cold water into the bath and dropped her in, face down. He held her head under and there were no bubbles. Nothing. Okay.

He wiped his hands and checked his appearance in the mirror over the basin. Not a mark on him.

The gun that fitted so snugly under his left armpit would have done the job faster, but then somebody might have heard and that might have meant shooting his way out of the building, which was no way to handle a little thing like a doll who tried to be too friendly.

He had touched nothing, only the body. He looked at the dark hair floating down there, and the clothes spreading in the water. A real doll.

He retrieved his hat and let himself out. Nobody had noticed his arrival, and nobody had any reason to notice his departure. Half past seven in the evening was sacred to 'Coronation Street', and he had been up there only for a few minutes.

They were heading west for the motorway at a very handsome rate.

'Suppose old Tommy did a crafty one on

you,' said Sam. 'I mean, you split up and he didn't know he was going to get clobbered … maybe he didn't reckon he owed you anything.'

'He owed me enough,' said Carrie curtly. 'It's no good to him where he is. I'm pretty damn sure Ossie Trent was in on it, Tommy didn't fence his stuff with anybody else that I ever heard him mention. It's got to be Ossie Trent. If you don't fancy the trip, Sam, take us on into Reading, and you can go back on the train. No hard feelings?'

Sam thought of his lousy little furnished room in Kilburn. He had invested time and energy in this lark already. He didn't think Carrie was going to collect any cash off Ossie Trent. But there was an outside chance that she might, and if she did he ought to be there.

'What's this business you were on about?' he said.

'A half share in a beauty parlour concession in a first class hotel, if you really must know. It's a gold mine.'

'That's nice,' he said. 'Where?'

'Ibiza. I have to come up with my share of the capital now or I'll lose the offer. That's why I've been rushing after Ossie Trent. Now you know it all, Sammie.'

'Room for me?' he said. 'I'm a versatile character.'

'What would you do?' she said. 'Sweep the floor of the salon? Let's be sensible about this, Sammie. When I collect from Ossie Trent you'll be on a percentage for your trouble. How's that?'

Sam grunted. He couldn't see himself getting bloody rich that way. 'Make it ten percent,' he said. 'Easy to reckon.'

Carrie patted his thigh, intimately, and he had to concentrate on his driving. Then he laughed. 'I've just remembered, I've still got the bathroom key – Nickie Preston will have to bust the door in ... they won't be liking us very much.'

'They tried to cut themselves in on something that didn't concern them,' said Carrie, 'and they came unstuck. We needn't weep for those two ... are you still with me, Sammie?'

'All the way,' said Sam.

12

Ossie did not intend to punish himself unduly in his country retreat. He kept a small supply of tinned food at the cottage, but he wasn't going to do any cooking; he might boil an egg and make tea or coffee, but that would be all; he was going to have his main meals out.

He refused to think of himself as a fugitive; he had merely taken a sensible precaution in the circumstances. He would keep clear of the London scene, and Harry would let him know what was happening. It was going to be all right.

The cottage was not much to look at, with its grey stone walls and little windows and sloping slate roof that needed repairing. But it had the essentials, including a phone, and its isolated position at the end of the common suited Ossie. Cars couldn't park on the common, and his nearest neighbours were usually a few old horses and cows on the free grazing. There was a track from the road that allowed him to drive his car into a shed beside the cottage.

Later in the evening he walked across the common and down into the town, and over the bridge to dinner at the 'Bear', and he promised himself he'd make the trip for breakfast each morning; the exercise would be good for him. Passing the time would be no difficulty. He wouldn't have to remain stuck in the cottage chewing his finger nails and pacing up and down. If Harry had anything to report he would ring at night when he knew Ossie would be in.

He enjoyed a very pleasant dinner, over which there was absolutely no need to hurry. He was not just passing through like most of the other diners, and he decided he could stand a week or two of this, making his own pace. There were plenty of places he could visit. He would work out some routes to west country towns where he knew he could get some decent meals in civilised surroundings.

And each night he would be back in the cottage in case Harry called. Already he was feeling more at ease. He was watching a small party at a nearby table, late arrivals like himself. A middle-aged couple with a girl in her early twenties, their daughter, it seemed. An attractive girl who was clearly bored with her parents. She had a wandering eye, and she put on that sexy pouting look as soon as she became aware of Ossie's interest.

Nothing could come of it. Just a bit of the old game. Reminding him that he was going to miss Laura for a while.

He strolled back through the town, and turned up across the common. There was a car parked up there along by the wood, well off the common, with no lights. The driver was taking something of chance, parking there, but he probably reckoned he was safe enough there, with his girl. The back seat of a car in the dark still had attractions, and the best of luck to them.

The garden gate squeaked and he made a mental note to oil it in the morning. He might do some other light chores, chop down some of the tall grass. Laura called it a jungle. He was remembering a week-end there with her, it had rained and they hadn't stirred much outside that bedroom up there until midday. She said the place had possibilities and he ought to spend some money on it.

He unlocked the front door. There was a tiny lobby with the stairs right there in front.

He reached round into the living-room and put the light on, and he froze instantly at what he saw, sitting across from the door, waiting for him.

'Come on in and sit down where I can see you,' said Don Vives.

Ossie Trent dropped into the chair that was pointed out to him, unable to take his eyes off the swarthy man in the dark suit with his hat in his lap; a compact and motionless figure, with watchful dark eyes.

This had to be the one Harry Fergus had talked about, the hard man, the imported hatchet-man. Ossie's faculties seemed to have abandoned him temporarily, and the first thing he was able to say was the fatuous question, 'How did you get in here?'

'Your back door's nothing but a joke,' said Don Vives. 'You didn't run far enough, mister.'

'I don't know you,' said Ossie, which also was not a very intelligent contribution.

'You don't need to know me,' said Vives. 'But you know why I'm here.'

Ossie rubbed his hands down his thighs, to stop them trembling. He glanced at the phone on the little table beside him.

'No,' said Vives. 'That wouldn't be a good thing to do. Let's talk business.'

'I can't think of any business I might have with you, whoever you are.' He had to play for time, keep talking while he worked out some way of out-witting this thug. 'I find it very embarrassing to speak to a man who refuses to give me his name, especially after he has broken into my house – burglary is not quite the most civilised of introductions, don't you agree? I would offer you a drink, but this is hardly a social occasion, is it?' There was a solid glass ashtray on a shelf. If he could distract the other's attention long enough to get hold of it – he crossed his legs and then uncrossed them again.

'Sit still, buddie,' said Don Vives.

'You must forgive me for appearing ill at ease,' said Ossie, 'but I am not in the habit of entertaining uninvited guests–' There was the table, he could shove it over into his visitor's lap and jump across the room to the back door and into the cover of the darkness outside … all he needed was the first move…

Don Vives shifted his hat from his lap, and showed his gun.

'You getting any ideas?' he said.

Ossie sat back in his chair, and lifted both hands in surrender.

'There's a contract out for you,' said Vives, 'and I'm the guy that got it, so here I am.

175

What made you think you could steal from the Boston Office and get away with it? Don't you have any sense at all?'

'It wasn't quite like that,' said Ossie.

'No? Then tell me how it was.'

'I didn't intend to steal anything,' said Ossie weakly. 'It was an unfortunate combination of circumstances.'

'You make with the words,' said Don Vives. 'Nobody puts the bite on the Boston Office.'

'The situation was confused,' said Ossie, and then added with the little dignity he had left, 'I assure you I am not a thief. I resent the suggestion.'

How much did they know?

'Okay,' said Don Vives. 'Now tell me about the stocks and bonds you were holding for Joey Rossi when he got whacked out.'

Ossie's insides turned over. 'There was nobody I knew who was available to take the stuff over,' he said. 'That was just the way it happened, with all the shooting going on … everybody was going into hiding…'

'You thought there wouldn't be any records,' said Vives. 'Let me tell you something you should have known for yourself, buddie – Joey Rossi kept good records, he knew where every last cent of his was, he was in the business and he didn't forget any of the details, he put them all down in his little book, and that little book shows what you owe us.'

Ossie Trent was doing some desperate mental calculations without coming up with any kind of an answer.

'They figured it out before they sent me over,' said Don Vives. 'Real businesslike; at the current rate of exchange you owe in English pounds fifty two grand and four centuries, to make it a nice round figure, and we're not charging you interest.'

'I can't pay that.' Ossie's voice had dwindled to a whisper. 'I don't have that kind of money–'

'You stole that kind,' said Vives. 'You stole it when you reckoned nobody was alive to know what you were doing. Joey Rossi gave you a break, a square deal, so when he's dead you rob him, that makes you something that crawled out of a sewer.'

'Please listen,' said Ossie.

'They sent me here to collect or else,' said Vives. 'I heard enough talk.'

'You must listen,' said Ossie and he wasn't play-acting. He had never felt more in earnest. 'Can't we come to some kind of an arrangement? You don't expect me to be holding that much money, it's not reasonable...'

He was pleading, and it wasn't just about the money. It was the 'or else' that had him shaking inside, this was the hatchet-man. Like Vince Flemmi.

'You have a suggestion?' said Vives politely.

'I can raise about twenty thousand,' said Ossie. 'I can let you have cheques on some of my accounts in London—'

'That leaves thirty two thousand and four hundred still dangling,' said Vives. 'You reckon that's a good offer?'

'It's the best I can do right away,' said Ossie. 'I can pay off the rest by instalments, you can explain that to them over there ... it will take a little time but I promise I can do it.'

'That's not even fifty percent,' said Vives. 'Maybe they won't think I did my job.'

'Most of my money is tied up,' said Ossie. 'If you give me time I can raise it, but I can give you cheques for twenty thousand that you can cash tomorrow, and I'll give you a letter of authority to show at the banks.'

'Write the cheques,' said Vives. 'Make them payable to Don Vives.'

Ossie had brought his case with him. In it were his cheque books and a few personal papers that went with him wherever his business took him. Don Vives let him unlock the case and then took it from him and emptied its contents on to the table.

'I don't own a gun,' said Ossie.

'Not much good to you in there, sport,' said Vives. 'If you have a gun you keep it handy, like this.' He held his gun trained on Ossie's middle. He watched Ossie write out three cheques on three banks, two for eight thousand and one for four; and he had to spell out his name for Ossie. Then the letter of authority to the bank managers.

The cheques would temporarily bankrupt him – unless he could somehow get rid of this thug and stop the cheques in the morning.

He put the cheques and the letter into an envelope and held it out. 'I think that completes our business for tonight, I hope you'll have a pleasant journey back to London.'

Don Vives slipped the envelope into his pocket, and sat down again. 'You might change your mind between now and tomorrow, so we'll stay together. I wouldn't like to think I might be handling any rubber cheques.'

'But you can't stay here all night,' said Ossie. 'It isn't necessary, those cheques won't bounce, I give you my word–'

–'I'm a careful guy,' said Vives. 'Sleep on

the floor if you like, makes no difference to me. I'll sit here and watch.'

Ossie resumed his seat. It was a hopeless situation to be in, and from the look of Don Vives he was quite prepared to sit in that chair all night, with his gun in his lap.

'Is it all right if I make some coffee?' said Ossie.

Don Vives just nodded, got up and went into the kitchen with him. When the saucepan was ready to be poured, Ossie had a crazy notion about swinging around and tossing the contents into that vigilant dark face. But Vives moved deftly in and held his arm in a tight grip.

'That would be a waste, buddie,' he said.

Ossie's hand shook as he poured the coffee into two mugs. There was the back door open, just a few feet away, and the dark garden. If he had any guts left he'd try it.

Don Vives steered him back into the living-room and made sure he carried both mugs. And told him again where he was to sit. Suddenly Ossie was feeling exhausted, as though he had run a couple of miles uphill.

'Who told you I was here?' he said. 'Was it Harry Fergus? Nobody else knew.'

'Think again,' said Don Vives. 'I'll give you a clue, she's a good-looking broad and she's very helpful. You make fair coffee.'

'Laura,' said Ossie softly. 'Oh my God, I didn't think of her...'

'Never trust a gabby doll,' said Vives. 'They always spill it. You've been shacking up with that one, lots of folks knew about it, so it was easy to get a line on her, and I called on her this very evening. I'll tell you the truth, buddie, if I'd had the time to spare I could have got myself laid then and there.'

Ossie glared at him. This was such a clumsy attempt to provoke him into some explosion. So he kept his mouth shut.

'She offered to ring you here and let you know I was coming,' said Vives. 'I couldn't have that, now could I? So I had to take good care of her. You follow me, buddie? She won't be making any more calls. Permanent.'

It was a few moments before the words actually registered.

'You mean you killed her?' said Ossie. 'You bastard!'

'Would you be waiting here for me?' said Vives. 'You would have been running again if you knew I was coming, check?'

Ossie thrust himself out of his chair, both fists clenched and raised, launching himself forward.

'No!' snapped Don Vives, and without

moving from his chair shot Ossie low in the belly.

Ossie doubled over, went to his knees and then face down on the floor. Only then did Don Vives move. Ossie was trying to lift himself up on his forearms. Vives planted a foot on his back and stamped him hard down.

'Johnny Scimona says to tell you goodbye, buddie...'

Ossie groaned at the searing hot pain stabbing in his belly. Don Vives bent over and fired the finishing shot, the traditional one in the back of the head.

Then he took the coffee mugs into the kitchen and rinsed them, wiping his prints off before stacking them in the rack. He collected his hat from the table, turned off the light and locked the door behind him. He walked briskly along the rough grass until he came to his car by the wall, and then he threw the key into the wood.

Twenty grand was nothing special in the mob's finances. He would cash the cheques in the morning. The important item was that he had taken care of that rat, Oswald Trent. Everybody knew it was a fatal thing to steal from the Office.

It was late by the time Carrie and Sam

reached the town, nearly half past eleven, and there were few pedestrians around to help them with local directions. In the wide main street they came across a youth who said the common was on his way home. He rode with them and pointed out where they would find the cottage. He said he didn't reckon they'd find anybody there because it was only used at week-ends. He was a nice friendly lad, and quite interested in Carrie. Perhaps he suspected they were looking for a quiet place to bed down, and he was ready to ride all the way with them.

Carrie thanked him and got rid of him.

The cottage was in darkness as Sam drove up the track, and when they got out he left their headlights on because he didn't fancy the look of the place. There was a shed alongside and the door was a poor fit, and Sam got a glimpse of the back of a car inside. A Mercedes. So the place wasn't empty.

There was no bell on the front door, just an old brass knocker, and Carrie hammered on it with vigour. Nobody answered and she banged again, and she used some coarse words as she waited. Sam sidled around to look at the back. Nobody was in, that was sure.

Seconds later the lights were on inside and

Sam was dragging the front door open. His voice shook.

'Come on in and look at this—'

Carrie followed him in and saw what lay on the floor by the table. She knelt and then whispered, 'I think it's Ossie Trent—'

'Plugged through the back of his head,' said Sam, 'and not long ago either—'

'It's Ossie Trent all right.' Carrie stood up.

'Listen,' said Sam, 'let's get the hell out of this – it's murder and it's nothing to do with us—'

'Don't be so stupid,' she said. 'That young chap we gave a lift to, he's going to remember us, he knows we were coming here – he'll yak his head off as soon as they find the body. Do you want to have the police chasing after us on a murder charge? I don't.'

'Bloody hell,' said Sam. 'What a mess.'

Carrie went over to the phone.

'You calling the fuzz?' he said.

'Of course,' she said. 'You hop out and put our lights off, and mind you come back, Sammie – I'm not going to be left with this all on my own.'

'I wouldn't think of it,' said Sam, which was not the strict truth. What a godawful night this was turning out to be, and it wasn't over by a long chalk. He went out and did as he was told. The temptation to push off was strong, but he knew Carrie wouldn't let him get far.

In less than half an hour the official business was under way, first with a Sergeant and a Constable, and a little later with an Inspector. Sam had been under police interrogation before, and he knew their explanation of how they had come to visit Little End at that late hour only to find a dead body was not going down too well.

There seemed to be little known locally about the late Oswald Trent. He was a business man from London, and the opening of the motorway had made the town almost a London suburb.

The atmosphere improved a little when the Inspector went through the leather case and found the cheque books. The stubs had been neatly filled in, and the last cheque from each book had that day's date: two for eight thousand pounds and one of four thousand, all made payable to a Don Vives.

'Twenty thousand,' said Carrie bitterly. Some of that could have been hers. 'I've never heard of Don Vives, Inspector, but I suggest you ought to be out looking for him.'

'Thank you,' said the Inspector politely.

'The thought had come to me.'

'The cheques were dated today,' said Sam helpfully. 'Maybe he didn't cash them yet.' And the Inspector gave him a nice encouraging smile as well.

They went down to the Station and made formal statements like law-abiding citizens anxious to do their duty. Carrie told part of the truth – that Oswald Trent owed her some money on a private debt, she had come down to the cottage to get it and she had found him dead, so she had phoned the police.

Sam told the complete truth, which was something of a record for him. He was Carrie's driver. He had got into the cottage through the busted back door and it had been busted before he got there, and there was this dead bloke on the floor. And that was all he knew about it – let them pick the bones out of it, they could never prove any different.

At last they were allowed to return to London, and their journey was done largely in a depressed silence.

'So bang goes your beauty parlour,' said Sam. 'That was rough luck, Carrie. Now we'll never know for sure if Ossie Trent was diddling you, and Tommy won't tell you.'

In one picturesque phrase Carrie made it clear what she thought about her husband.

Sam reflected for a moment. 'Y'know,' he said, 'if we'd got there a bit earlier we might have run into something – and you could have done some clever stuff with your little gun, you told Nickie Preston what a good shot you are–'

'I was fooling,' she said. 'I didn't have any bullets in the gun.'

'Oh my Gawd!' said Sam. 'You took a chance – we could have been clobbered!'

'Now belt up,' she said. 'I want to get some sleep.'

When they stopped outside her flat he roused her. 'I'm hungry as hell,' he said hopefully. 'I haven't had a bite all night.'

'You can come on up,' she said wearily. 'I'll give you some food, Sammie, but don't expect anything else.'

The eternal optimist, Sam went up with her. His theory was that once you got a foot inside a girl's pad you were practically in bed with her. Carrie cooked him bacon and eggs, and he had to eat alone. When she went into her bedroom he heard the key turn. So he didn't get a nibble at anything private on the side, and after all his exertions on her behalf.

There was no justice in it. He tapped on her door and she called out and told him what he could do with himself. He replied in similar terms. It was an undignified ending to nothing at all. Bloody women. Sam thought of his immediate future and found it bleak indeed.

To even things up he took Carrie's car when he left. He could flog it under the counter for a hundred and fifty or so. The prospect cheered him. There was always a way out if you used your loaf.

Don Vives presented himself with one of the cheques for eight thousand at the Mayfair branch of a bank. If they made any fuss he was prepared to give them a line of soft talk and remove himself. This was just a try-on. Why pass up the cash if it was there to be picked up?

He was received with a courtesy that flattered him. It was so unlike any treatment he ever got in any city bank in the States. Eight thousand pounds in large notes, fifties? Whatever the gentleman preferred. No trouble at all. Perhaps Mr Vives would care to wait in the manager's office while the money was being made up?

Nice guys, English bankers. Don Vives followed the polite cashier into a small room at the end of the counter. There were two characters waiting in there for him – young and sharp-looking guys.

'Mr Don Vives?' said one of them.

'That's right.' Don Vives always reckoned he could smell the fuzz a couple of blocks away. He backed off and went for his gun.

He was very quick, but not quick enough, and there were two of them. For the first time in his active career he was jumped and slammed against the wall with a knee in his belly.

He was efficiently relieved of his gun, and a forearm across his windpipe eliminated any wish he might have had to make a speech. They were very rough young guys.

'They dug two bullets out of Oswald Trent, Mr Don Vives. This gun fired them, correct?'

Although the pressure had been now removed from his throat, Don Vives was in no mood for talk. The Boston Office didn't reach this far. They ran things differently in this lousy little country.

He didn't look very dangerous when they took him away. Sam Harris read about it in the evening paper. And so did Carrie. She was grieved beyond words that she couldn't think of any way of getting hold of any of that money.

Weeks later she was still looking for Sam Harris, the thieving little red-headed swine, and Sam was making very sure that she didn't find him. Survival was everything, and Sam was good at that.

P.N